dark blue

dark blue

color me lonely

melody carlson

NAVPRESS ®

For a free catalog
of NavPress books & Bible studies call
1-800-366-7788 (USA) or 1-800-839-4769 (Canada).

www.NavPress.com

TH1NK Books is an imprint of NavPress. TH1NK is a registered trademark of NavPress. Absence of ® in connection with marks of NavPress or other parties does not indicate an absence of registration of those marks.

ISBN 10: 1-57683-529-4
ISBN 13: 978-1-57683-529-6

Cover design by David Carlson Design
Cover image by Image Source
Creative Team: Jay Howver, Erin Healy, Darla Hightower, Pat Reinheimer

This is a work of fiction. The characters, incidents, and dialogues are products of the author's imagination and are not to be construed as real. Any resemblance to actual events or persons, living or dead, is entirely coincidental.

Published in association with the literary agency of Sara A. Fortenberry.

Scripture taken from the *New King James Version.* Copyright © 1982 by Thomas Nelson, Inc. Used by permission. All rights reserved.

Carlson, Melody.
  Dark blue : color me lonely, a novel / by Melody Carlson.-- 1st ed.
    p. cm. -- (True colors ; bk. 1)
Summary: Two sophomore girls, best friends since kindergarten, grow apart when one wants new friends and decides the other is a popularity liability.
  ISBN 1-57683-529-4
  [1. Best friends--Fiction. 2. Friendship--Fiction. 3. High schools--Fiction. 4. Schools--Fiction. 5. Christian life--Fiction.] I. Title.
  PZ7.C216637Dar 2004
  [Fic]--dc22
                                        2003022054

Printed in the United States of America

6 7 8 9 10 11 12 / 11 10 09 08 07

Other Books by Melody Carlson

Moon White (NavPress)
Bright Purple (NavPress)
Faded Denim (NavPress)
Bitter Rose (NavPress)
Blade Silver (NavPress)
Fool's Gold (NavPress)
Burnt Orange (NavPress)
Pitch Black (NavPress)
Torch Red (NavPress)
Deep Green (NavPress)
Dark Blue (NavPress)
DIARY OF A TEENAGE GIRL *series* (Multnomah)
DEGREES *series* (Tyndale)
Crystal Lies (WaterBrook)
Finding Alice (WaterBrook)
Three Days (Baker)
On This Day (WaterBrook)

To Kimi Hamilton and Allie Nemeth,

thanks for sharing your ideas with me.

mc

one

JORDAN FERGUSON *USED* TO BE MY BEST FRIEND. NOW SHE MAKES ME sick. Just hearing her name called out in first period English or seeing her flitting down the hall with her lame new friends makes me want to hurl. Really!

And comments like, "Oh, Jordan, I totally love your hair today," or, "Hey, Jordan, that outfit is really hot," actually make me want to hit something. I mean *puh-leeze*, these are the exact same girls Jordan and I *used* to make fun of. Behind their backs anyway—it's not like we were ignorant. At least I'm not. I can't speak for Jordan—not anymore.

Not that I ever did speak for Jordan. No, she's always been perfectly capable of doing that herself. The sorry truth is, whether I liked it or not, she often spoke for me too. I guess it all started way back in kindergarten. My parents had recently divorced and I thought their problems were all my fault. As a result I think I was feeling pretty insecure and probably scared too. I didn't want to talk to anyone and made a point of hanging out on the sidelines and keeping my little mouth shut. But one day our kindergarten teacher Miss March asked, "Who wants to play with the puppet theater next?" And even though I was dying to put my hand inside of that plump pink Miss Piggy puppet, I couldn't utter a single word. I nearly fell over when this tiny blonde girl wearing a mint-green My Little Pony sweatshirt walked over and took me by the hand.

"Kara Hendricks and I want to do the puppets now," she said in this great big voice that totally contradicted her size. Jordan was the smallest girl in the class back then. Even now she's barely five feet tall in her socks. But how she actually knew, at the age of five, not only my first but also my last name was a complete mystery to me. So naturally I didn't argue with her. I even managed to find my voice once I was safely behind the puppet theater curtain and my hand was tucked into the bright-green Kermit the Frog puppet. Naturally, Jordan wanted Miss Piggy for herself. And who was I to question the girl who helped me step outside of myself for a change? Not having Miss Piggy seemed a pretty small sacrifice. After that, Jordan did most of the talking for both of us, especially during that first year. Oh, I would talk to her, but only in this quiet mousy voice. Then she would speak to the teacher or a classmate or whoever until my wants and needs were perfectly clear. It's like I was the hand puppet and she was the puppeteer. Still, her outgoing personality made life much easier for me.

Fortunately, I did get better at speaking, over time. But I've never been what you might call an assertive or even confident person. And I would never in a million years want to speak in public on purpose. Jordan, on the other hand, loved her speech class last year and even joined the debate team, and she was only a freshman! But I don't get it. I mean why would anyone willingly put themselves into a position where they have to speak in front of an audience *and* argue about something? How whacked out is that?

Still, I admit that I admired her for it. I thought she was the bravest and coolest person I knew. And throughout our freshman year in high school, just last year, I was totally thankful that I had

Jordan Ferguson to share a locker, walk down the halls, eat lunch, and just basically hang with. She was like my security blanket. Well, that and a lot more.

I suppose that's why losing her like this is so freaking crappy. Not that I'll ever admit *that*. Not to her or anyone else in this moronic school. As it is, my life already sucks. I don't need anyone's stupid pity to add to my stinking pile of misery. Besides, I do a pretty good job of feeling sorry for myself.

"What's up with you and Jordan?" my teenybopper sister asked the other day. "How come she never comes 'round here anymore?"

Naturally, Bree *would* miss Jordan. She thinks Jordan's the coolest thing next to (gag me) Britney Spears. Just the same, I rolled my eyes at her and said, "Probably because you're such a total stink bomb. Poor Jordan just couldn't take your smell anymore."

Of course, this led to a rip-snorting argument about hygiene and fashion and a bunch of other things Bree and I don't quite agree on. Turned out to be a good distraction—Bree hasn't mentioned Jordan's absence since. Still, I'm sure she privately wonders. You'd think my mom might wonder too, but as usual she's so into her own world that she is totally clueless about mine. So what's new?

But I guess I sort of wish my mom would ask me about it. Now tell me that's not weird, since I usually don't want to talk (I mean *talk*) to my mom about anything besides lunch money or whose turn it is to clean the kitchen. I guess that just shows how completely desperate I am.

I sort of feel like I'm drowning here, and I just keep wishing that someone—anyone—would toss me a life preserver, or even a rope . . . maybe to hang myself with. Because I really need someone to talk to. The pathetic thing is, the only person I've ever poured my heart out to before, the only one who's ever listened or attempted to give me answers, the only one who knew how to make me feel better, just doesn't give a rip.

As furious as I am with Jordan, and as much as I can't stand the very sight of her, I still miss her friendship more than I imagined possible, and I think I'd do almost anything to get her back. As lame as it sounds, even to me, there's a great big gaping hole in my life right now. And I feel more alone than ever.

Not to mention scared.

two

LAST FALL, AT THE BEGINNING OF OUR FRESHMAN YEAR, JORDAN announced that she was going to try out for cheerleading.

"Have you totally lost your mind?" I asked her.

"No, I think it'd be fun."

"Oh, sure. Wearing one of those stupid dinky outfits that make your thighs look fat, standing in front of the entire school, and letting someone drop you on your head. Big-time fun!"

"Oh, Kara, you're such a killjoy. You need to learn to lighten up a little." Then she got that look, that I-have-a-plan-for-your-life kind of look. "And to that end, I have decided that you should try out with me."

"Okay, Jordan, now I *know* you've lost it." I studied this girl who'd been my best friend for the best part of eight years. I say "the best part" because we did experience one major fallout during fourth grade when I called her "shrimp bait" while shooting hoops with some boys I wanted to impress (including Joshua Horsinger, the boy Jordan had a major crush on at the time). Anyway, she was so embarrassed and furious that she didn't forgive me for two whole weeks. The most miserable two weeks of my entire life. Well, up until now. And it wasn't like I didn't immediately apologize either. I wrote her about a hundred "I'm sorry" notes and gave her my most valuable Beanie Baby (Magic, the beautiful iridescent dragon). And I bought her a giant box of her favorite movie candy, Milk Duds, and finally got down on my knees in front of God and everyone on the blacktop of the Fairview Elementary playground and begged her to forgive me. Thankfully, she did.

But as I stood there that crisp autumn day last year, actually considering what it was that she was asking me to do, which was to stand before hundreds of cynical kids, mostly older than me and probably just hoping that someone like me would make a total fool of herself . . . well, suddenly my lifelong buddy seemed like a complete and somewhat frightening stranger to me.

"Jordan, you know I'd never be able to do that," I told her. "I'd totally freak. It'd be a complete disaster. You've got to be kidding. *Right?*"

She folded her arms across her chest and just shook her head.

"No way." I stood firm.

"Come on, Kara," she pleaded. "Please. I don't want to do this alone."

"I just can't, Jordan." I sighed, feeling a bit sick to my stomach just thinking of what she was asking me. "I'd honestly rather strip down to my underwear, put a paper bag over my head, and run screaming through a pep assembly."

"Really?" She looked hopeful. "Then how about doing *that* for tryouts?"

"This is ridiculous, Jordan. You know there's no way on earth that I can do something like this."

She frowned. "Yeah, I was afraid you'd say that." Then she shrugged. "I guess I'll just have to go solo."

Now I just stared at her. "No. Way."

"Way. That's what I'm gonna do."

"Are you serious?"

Now she made her pouty face. "Yeah, since my very best friend has left me no choice, I guess I'll just have to do it all by myself. All by my little lonesome."

For the first time that I can remember, Jordan's guilt trip didn't work on me. As bad as I hated to disappoint my best friend, I knew there was absolutely no way, short of a lobotomy, that I could do this thing. Now I wouldn't exactly say I have a real honest-to-goodness social phobia that requires medication for me to function properly, but I think it's probably close. I'm pretty sure that I am one of the shiest girls at Jackson High. Without Jordan bolstering my confidence all these years, I would've probably just disappeared into the background long ago. But even though I owed Jordan big time, I knew there was absolutely no way I could go through cheerleading tryouts without humiliating both of us. I think I honestly believed that my refusal to participate might discourage her enough to give up this totally lame idea. Unfortunately, it did not.

So being a good friend, I accompanied her to the gym to sign up for tryouts, and then I even waited in the bleachers while she and about thirty other giggling girls learned these stupid cheers and dorky routines. And being a good friend, I even helped her practice those stupid cheers and dorky routines. And I even gave her some pretty useful critique too, like how it might look better if she held her fingers tightly together, slightly cupped. I'd seen other cheerleaders doing that. But when the big day came, Jordan Ferguson was *not* picked to be a cheerleader.

I have never told her that I didn't vote for her or that I secretly rejoiced when her name was not included in the intercom announcement of new cheerleaders. Instead, I pretended to be truly heartbroken for her. I even took her out for a supersize hot fudge sundae after school. She'd been dieting all week in order to look better in the shorts outfit she'd bought for tryouts. I figured she was entitled to a pig-out pity party.

"You were totally great today," I told her as we gorged ourselves. At least *that* was the truth. Jordan really had done a fantastic job in front of those hundreds of gawking high-school kids. I was honestly dumbfounded that she was *not* picked. I had been freaking all afternoon, certain that my best friend was going to leave me behind for her new life as a cheerleader. Now I may not be an expert in the subject of cheerleading, but I knew enough to see that Jordan had performed the routine flawlessly, smiled beautifully, and jumped just as high as any of the girls who were selected. Besides that, Jordan looked exactly like a cheerleader should: petite and blonde and perky and cute. Everything that I am not nor ever will be.

Still, she just glumly shook her head. "I should've listened to you, Kara. What was I thinking?"

"Hey, you did your best," I assured her. "And, really, you looked way better than any of them." I pushed my empty dish away and groaned. "Way better than that stupid Betsy Mosler. I cannot believe that she got picked. Honestly, Jordan, I think you were robbed. Maybe someone stuffed the ballot box."

She smiled now. "Yeah, that's probably what happened. Maybe Betsy bribed kids to vote for her."

"Yeah, or maybe all the boys voted for Ashley Crow just to see her bounce when she does her leaps."

And so we laughed and made fun of all the new cheerleaders and life returned to normal.

Of course, that was then and this is now. And normal doesn't live here anymore.

three

So there I was, just standing in line at the cafeteria, trying to decide whether to have a chef salad or a cheeseburger, and Jordan breaks the news that she was going to try out for cheerleading again. I turned to see if she was really serious. But I could tell by the steely look in her blue eyes that she was not to be dissuaded. So I kept my mouth shut, ordered the cheeseburger, and prayed (yes, I literally prayed to God himself) that my very best friend would fall flat on her face, make a total fool of herself, and give up this cheerleading nonsense for good. Wasn't it enough that she was on the debate team, had made honor roll, and excelled in gymnastics last year? What more did she want?

Maybe it's *because* I prayed that Jordan did so well. Maybe her success was God's way of getting even with me for being so hopelessly selfish. Because not only did Jordan get picked, she was the absolute hit of tryouts. It's like everyone in Jackson High just totally loved her.

And that's when my life began to deteriorate.

"Can you believe it?" she shrieked when we met by our locker after school. I felt an autumn breeze drifting through the open-air locker bay, and although it was about seventy degrees in the shade, a distinct chill ran through me.

I forced what I'm sure must've looked like a pretty poor excuse for a smile. "Congratulations, Jordan. You did it."

"Thanks." Then she turned to the millions of adoring fans who were obsessed with congratulating her, slapping her on the back, and giving her ridiculous two thumbs-up. Naturally, she flashed her best Colgate smile as she graciously told them all "thank you." You'd have thought she'd won an Oscar or something.

"Way to go, Ferguson," said Brett Hawkins with an appreciative nod. "Looking good."

"You did great," said Shawna Frye, another cheerleader and my old nemesis from sixth grade — she was always trying to steal Jordan from me. "It's no surprise that you made it, Jordan. Welcome to the team!"

"Thanks!" That flashy smile again. I wondered if she'd lightened her teeth especially for this day.

"Hey, Ferguson!" yelled Amber Elliot, head cheerleader and mouthiest girl at Jackson High. "Wait up. We got some celebrating to do, girlfriend."

Jordan turned to me with a pained expression. "Oh, that's right, Kara. There's some kind of party for the new cheerleaders right now."

I just shrugged like it was no big deal. "Hey, that's okay. I'll catch you later."

"Yeah. I'll call."

But she didn't. I hate to admit that I actually waited by the phone, because really I was just doing my geometry homework. But Jordan never called. She never emailed. She never dropped by. Nothing. Nada. Zip. Zero.

The next day, I stupidly waited on the corner where we usually meet before school. I knew that was probably an irrational move, since it seemed my life was over. But then I remembered how

Jordan always accuses me of being so negative, so I decided to take the positive approach and even managed to talk myself into believing that she would be there just like usual. But, of course, she never showed up. I'm sure that was the exact moment when I began to feel fairly certain that it was over between us. The nagging, churning feeling had started in the pit of my stomach the night before, gnawing on me like a hungry rat trying to eat me alive, but now it seemed to take over my entire being. I felt like I was actually getting physically sick. Since it looked like I'd be late anyway, I even considered going back home and claiming I had the flu. I knew I had *something*.

But still clinging to the tiniest shred of hope, I decided to do the brave thing—the thing that Jordan would do under these same circumstances (not that she's ever been in these circumstances). But I decided to proceed. I hurried past the security gates and through the front door, by myself, making it to my English class just as the last bell rang. I didn't even have time to stop by my locker first. Coming in late forced me to take a seat right up front, but maybe that was good because I never had to actually look at Jordan, who usually sits in the back row, plus I was able to leave quickly.

From there I managed to make it to economics class, but by then I felt like someone had pulled the plug on me as I slumped into an empty seat in the back of the stuffy room. I pretended to listen as Mr. Lee droned on and on about stocks and bonds and stupid financial things that no one in their right mind gives a flying fig about.

Like a zombie I maneuvered through my next class. Find a desk, sit down, look attentive, don't keep looking at the clock. *Just let this day end,* I kept telling myself as I walked alone down the hall. *Just let this day end.* Only when I went to art did I feel like I could almost breathe again. I allowed my mind to take a slight vacation from grief as I absently worked on a pathetic sketch of my Doc Marten sandal. Even my shoes looked like they were frowning.

I never even ran into Jordan until lunchtime and then, to my surprise, she acted like everything was just fine. Peachy even.

"Hey, Kara," she said with what seemed to me an increasingly white smile. What was she using on her teeth anyway? "What's up?" she asked, as if nothing had changed.

"What's up?" I stupidly echoed back, obviously regressing to my kindergarten phase where Jordan took charge of all conversations.

"Are you okay, Kara?"

"Okay?"

She frowned now. "Really, you don't look too good. Are you sick or something?"

I shook my head. "No, I'm okay."

Then, chattering on like everything was normal, she apologized for not meeting me before school, claiming that her little sister, Leah, had been experiencing a middle-school meltdown.

"I don't know what gets into that girl's head," said Jordan as we got in the lunch line. "She had this zit, just one little, tiny, barely noticeable zit on her chin, and she was just totally freaked. It's like it was cancer or something."

"Uh-huh," I nodded, thinking I knew exactly how Leah felt.

"Hey, Jordan!" called Amber Elliot from a nearby table—*the popular table*, or so the kids who sit there like to believe. "Come sit with us."

I felt a tightness growing in my throat as I selected a cup of vegetable soup and a bottle of juice. Somehow I thought perhaps liquids would go down more easily today. Then, like a dummy, I followed Jordan over to the "popular" table. Fortunately, or not, there were still a couple of available seats. No one said a single word to me as I sat down next to Jordan. Not only did they silently ignore me, but I could feel their eyes on me—not staring, but these furtive glances that feel almost worse. And I knew what they were thinking. *She doesn't belong here with us. Who does she think she is, anyway?* But Jordan seemed oblivious as she chatted and joked with her new friends. Before long I began to feel invisible. But not the good kind of invisible where people simply can't see you. It was more like the kind of invisible where someone has spinach in her teeth but no one says anything. Just the same, I suppose I was somewhat relieved to be ignored. Attention was the last thing I wanted right now.

Somehow I managed to slurp down part of my pathetic-looking liquid lunch before I mumbled a lame-sounding excuse and picked up my tray to casually exit. Naturally, on this day, of all days, my tray began to tilt precariously and the half-empty (or half-full, depending on how you look at it) cup of soup went sliding directly toward Jordan's lap.

She let out a bad word and leaped to her feet as the brown-orange mix of soup and juice coated her light khaki pants.

"Smooth move, Hendricks!" taunted Amber.

"I'm sorry, Jordan," I mumbled as I handed her a slightly used napkin.

"What a klutz," said Betsy Mosler.

Shawna Frye made a face. "Disgusting! That's gonna stink, Jordan."

Jordan was still unsuccessfully trying to blot her soup-soaked pants clean while I just stood there feeling like the village idiot. I expected the girls at the table to get up and start throwing stones and rotten vegetables at me any minute now.

"Hey, I've got a spare pair of jeans in my locker," said Shawna. "I'm sure they'll be a little big for you. What are you, Jordan, a size one?"

Jordan flashed that smile at her. "Oh, thanks, Shawna, that'd be great. I'm sure they'll fit fine."

So before I could say anything or do any more damage, Shawna led my *ex*-best friend away.

"Way to go, Kara," said Betsy loud enough for half the cafeteria to hear, even over the loud music. "With friends like you, who needs enemies?"

I wanted to ask Betsy why she couldn't think of anything more clever to say, but of course, I kept my mouth shut as I walked away from that stupid, snooty table. With my eyes downcast like I was looking for spare change on the floor, I deposited my messy tray. I made my way to the nearest exit, feeling as if I were wading through a sea of Jell-O, and vowed to never return to the cafeteria again. From now on I would brown-bag it with the rest of the losers who were too intimidated to face the tyrannies of the lunch line and cafeteria. Life as I'd known it was officially over.

four

IT FEELS INCREDIBLY LAME TO CARE THIS MUCH ABOUT SOMEONE. AND I'M embarrassed to admit that I have actually cried over losing Jordan. Sheesh, it's not like I'm a lesbian or anything. It's just that she's been my best friend for, like, forever. And I honestly don't know how to function without her. I am such a loser.

"What's up with you?" she asks me a couple of days later as we stand in front of our locker.

"Me?" I stare at her like she's a complete stranger.

"You're acting so weird lately." She reaches up to get her biology book.

"*I'm* acting weird?"

Then she pauses to really look at me. "You just seem different, Kara. Are you okay?"

Why does she keep asking if *I'm* okay? And what do you say when your *ex*-best friend, who has turned into someone else, asks you if *you're* okay? Naturally, not feeling terribly clever, I say nothing.

So she just shakes her head and slams the locker shut. Obviously she hasn't noticed that I haven't retrieved my own notebook yet. But then why would she?

"Hey, Jordan," calls Shawna. "Did you hear we're going to practice outside today?"

Then Jordan and Shawna walk off together, discussing something as insipid as shoe colors. Jordan never even looks back.

At the end of the day, I notice that all of Jordan's things are missing from our locker. At first I am shocked and assume that someone
has broken into it. This happens at our school occasionally. And
sometimes the vice principal does locker searches when he suspects
someone's smuggled drugs onto campus. One time we even had a
police dog sniff around, but he didn't find anything. These thoughts
are going through my head, but then I notice a lime-green Post-it
note stuck on the inside of the door.

"Sharing lockers with Shawna now. Closer to the gym and better for practice. Jordan."

That is it. *Okay,* I tell myself, *it's really over now.* I wad up the
note, stuff it into a pocket of my backpack, and head toward the exit.
It feels like I'm walking in a dream now, like nothing is real. Or perhaps I'm not real. Maybe everyone else is real, everyone except me.

I blankly observe the kids milling around, laughing, joking,
teasing. Girls in groups, guys in groups, some couples hanging onto
each other like they can't bear to let go, a few even making out. But
I just keep moving along by myself. Like I am in some kind of bub-
ble, alone and apart and separate from everyone else.

No one says a single word to me as I walk down the hall. In fact,
I don't think anyone has said much of anything to me these last few
days. Now that I think about it, I'm sure the only reason anyone
ever spoke to me before was because of Jordan. I feel like I am nothing without her. And I wonder how I will survive three years of this
kind of nothingness in high school. I have never felt so alone or
utterly hopeless in my life.

I head straight to our apartment complex just a few blocks from
school. It's not exactly a lovely abode, with its boring off-white

stucco exterior and "modern" architectural touches, but at least it's a retreat of sorts. I walk upstairs and enter our sterile-looking living room—my mom's into "contemporary" furnishings, which basically means cold and uncomfortable. The couch is an asymmetrical design of pewter-colored leather and looks about as inviting as a rock. This is flanked by a couple of metal-and-leather chairs in a garish shade of red, which I assume is meant to complement the piece of modern art that dominates this rather small room. Now I must say this artwork is one of the few items in our home that doesn't set my teeth on edge. It's loud and colorful, but at least there's a warmth to it, or so I like to imagine. And it was created by my dad. I suppose that might have something to do with why I like it. I go over and turn on the little chrome spotlight, which really makes the colors pop. My mom doesn't like to leave any lights on in the apartment since she's an electricity conservation freak. But sometimes I get up in the middle of the night and come in here and turn on that little light and just look at the painting. It's an abstract that I don't really understand, but somehow it usually comforts me.

But not today. I flick off the spotlight and, like a whipped puppy, I slink off to my room. I close the door and wish it had a deadbolt. Not that Bree or my mom will want to come in here. But I just do not want to be disturbed—not by anyone. *Like anyone wants to disturb me.*

I flop onto my bed and cry all over again. I wonder how long I can keep this up. It's not as if someone has died, for pity's sake. Why am I crying like a big baby over losing a stupid friend? I know I should be more mature than this. I yell at myself and say, "Just grow up!" and, "Get over it, you moron!" But my verbal abuse doesn't work. Even though I know it's totally stupid to care this much, to be hurt this badly, I simply don't know how to stop the pain.

I sit up and take a deep breath, telling myself that I can't go on like this. And for a moment, I honestly consider praying to God for help. Not that God and I really have much going on these days. Come to think of it, praying was what got me into this mess. And the truth is, I've only been to church a few dozen times in my entire life, and that's always been with Jordan's family. *Jordan's family!* Oh, the mere thought of Jordan's family—my second family—pushes me right over the edge again. And I begin to cry even harder than before.

It's like I can picture them all standing right there at the foot of my bed, and each one is waving to me. First I see Jordan's cool and laid-back parents. I think they actually used to be hippies back in the seventies, although they swear they never did drugs. They've always let me call them Tom and Cindy, and they've always welcomed me into their big, old, rambling home as if it were my own. Tom is usually dressed in shabby sweaters and wrinkled slacks, and he manages the oldies radio station in town. When Cindy isn't working part-time as a counselor, she's wearing overalls and painting cool pictures or digging in her huge garden. I can even see Jordan's older sister, Abbie, looking stylish as ever in the latest fad, and I remember the way she used to help us do our hair and nails and stuff when we were still in middle school. And then there's Leah, just a little younger than Bree, and then little Tommy, Jordan's sweet but pesky little brother. All of them are smiling and waving and saying, "Goodbye."

"I cannot take this!" I sob into my already soaking-wet pillow. "It's not fair."

Somehow, I mercifully fall asleep and don't wake up until I hear Mom calling me to come answer the phone. Shocked that anyone would call me, I wander out to the kitchen, blinking like a mole at the light as I pick up the phone receiver. (No, we do not have a cordless phone like everyone else in the civilized world. Our old-fashioned device is securely attached by a stretched-out cord to the wall right over the breakfast bar where everyone can listen in.)

"Hello?" I say in a voice that cracks slightly.

"Kara?"

"Jordan?" I feel an atom-sized spark of hope in my heart.

"I just thought I should call you and explain."

"Explain?"

"You know, about the locker thing. It's nothing personal, you know. It's just more convenient to share with Shawna now. It's by the gym, you know. And we have so many practices."

"Oh, that's okay," I lie.

"I thought you'd understand."

Yeah, I understand, all right.

"I still want us to be friends, Kara. I don't want you to think I'm dumping you. You don't, do you?"

"Well . . . "

"I mean, I know I've got some new friends now. It's just the way it goes with cheerleading and stuff. But I still consider you my best friend."

"Really?" A strange sensation washes over me. I think it is hope.

"Yeah. I mean we've been friends for, like, forever, Kara. Something like that can't change overnight."

I sigh in relief.

"But you've got to accept that I have new friends too. And you've got to try harder to be friendly to them, Kara."

"Be friendly?" I feel a tightness in my chest again. It's like someone has wrapped a leather strap around me and is steadily cinching it in.

"Yeah. I know they can be a little, well, you know. So I'm thinking you'll just have to make a bigger effort. Okay?"

Okay, I'm thinking. *Yeah, sure, okay. I'll just make a bigger effort. You bet!* "Uh, I'm not sure if I really know how to do that," I say uneasily. But at least that's honest.

"Oh, come on, Kara. You just need to smile more and laugh at their jokes and stuff. Just loosen up and don't take life so seriously all the time."

I consider this. "Yeah, maybe."

"And I haven't seen you around anywhere at lunchtime. Where have you been hiding, anyway?"

"Just around." I don't tell her about the secluded porch steps I recently discovered behind the art department.

"Well, why don't you make sure that you're *around* where I am tomorrow? It's going to be pretty hard to keep being your friend if I can never even find you."

"Okay," I agree meekly, experiencing a kindergarten flashback. "I'll meet you in the cafeteria tomorrow."

"Good." I can hear the smile in her voice now and I think, *Okay, maybe I have been overreacting about this whole thing. What—am I having PMS or something?* This is Jordan, after all. Why would she want to hurt me?

So I hang up the phone and then actually help my mom fix dinner. No big deal, really, since she's already got a frozen pizza sitting on the counter. But I do peel some carrots and cucumbers and de-string some celery to make a fairly nice-looking plate of veggies to go with it.

"You okay, honey?" she asks as I stir some ranch-dip mix into some mayonnaise for the veggies.

"Yeah, I guess so."

Then she calls for Bree to come and we sit down at the Formica-covered breakfast bar. As usual, we eat without saying much. The three of us sit facing our tiny kitchen with its stark white cabinets as we share our "deluxe" pizza, which tastes a bit like cardboard. It's a good thing I thought to add some veggies.

I try not to think about what's going on at the Ferguson's home right now, but I'm guessing they're all sitting around their big oak table and eating something really wonderful like homemade spaghetti or maybe even lasagna, and laughing a lot. Still, I'm imagining that I'll be back there with them before too long. Maybe by the weekend even.

After dinner, I return to my room and finish my homework. I even take some time to straighten my things and hang up some clothes. Lately, every time I get home from school, being depressed and upset, I've just thrown clothes and stuff down and left them to pile up wherever they landed. Fortunately, my mom, a neat freak when it comes to the rest of our apartment, isn't one of those types who does regular room inspections. Her philosophy is that it's my room and if I want to live like a slob, it's my problem. I can handle that. But actually, it was getting pretty awful in here, and it was even beginning to bug me.

Then, feeling more hopeful than I've felt all week, I take special care selecting what I think is my coolest outfit. Jordan actually picked all the pieces out when we were doing back-to-school shopping just a few weeks ago. I can't believe it's been only a few weeks! This outfit includes a pair of great jeans that fit perfectly and actually look pretty good on my overly long legs, as well as a T-shirt that cost way more than any earthly T-shirt should cost, but Jordan assured me it was worth it. Even so, I had to rip off the price tag before my mom figured it out. The T-shirt will be topped with this short cream-colored sweater we found on sale at the Gap. The bulkiness of the sweater helps to disguise my less-than-well-endowed chest, which used to be my greatest burden—but that was before this whole upset with Jordan.

Now that my wardrobe is pretty much settled (although I keep second-guessing myself) I stare into my dresser mirror and prepare to do a critical evaluation. Any new zits trying to develop? Anything I should attempt to fix? I'm still wondering how Jordan got her teeth so white. But, no, I look pretty much the same as usual. Ordinary and boring. Then I remind myself that Jordan would tell me to "think positively."

Okay, my long, dark brown hair is all right, I guess, probably my best asset, at least when I care for it properly. I give my head a sexy shake like I'm starring in a Pantene commercial and feel satisfied that it's fairly thick and perfectly straight with a natural shine to it. Jordan has always said she'd kill for my hair. Hers is blonde and cut just above her shoulders. It's slightly thin with a little bit of natural curl on the ends, but it looks good on her and seems to fit with her pixie-like face, which is something I envy. My face, on the other hand, feels too big for my body, and my facial features are not outstanding, although Abbie always said I had good lips—whatever that means. I pucker them up now and attempt to smile, but to me they just look like plain old lips.

I study my eyes next. Unfortunately, they're pretty puffy from all the crying I've done lately. But at least I have good lashes. They're fairly thick and dark, and I don't even need to use mascara, although Abbie always said I should anyway. I'm sorry to say my eye color is rather boring. My mom says it's hazel like my dad's, but it looks like a muddy mix of green and brown to me. I sometimes toy with the idea of getting those tinted contacts, maybe in teal, but my mom is not in favor of this idea. And right now, after my crying jag, my eyes look red and bloodshot. I sure hope they'll look better by lunchtime tomorrow.

Suddenly, I remember a trick that Abbie taught us—how to use cucumber slices on your eyes to reduce puffiness. I've seen her do it before but haven't tried it myself. So I depart from this pitiful inventory of my less-than-wonderful appearance to retrieve some cucumber slices from the refrigerator. Our apartment is dark and silent now. It appears that Bree and Mom have already gone to bed.

Finally, I get ready for bed myself. I place the cool cucumber slices over my puffy eyelids and tell myself to breathe deeply and think happy thoughts. I also tell myself that everything will return to normal soon, probably tomorrow. I even remind myself of one of Jordan's old seventies posters. It says: "Today is the first day of the rest of your life." Yes, I feel certain that things will be better.

But then, I've been tricked before.

five

ALL MORNING I FEEL NERVOUS, ANTICIPATING WHAT WILL HAPPEN AT lunch. I tell myself not to be so neurotic, but it does no good. It seems the only time I actually relax and forget about everything these days is during art class. It's like I can almost be myself in there.

Despite Jordan's opinion on art class—she thinks kids who take it are either freaks or geeks or just plain losers—I've decided I actually like it. A lot. This kind of surprises me since I've never considered myself to be particularly artistic, although I do keep a sketch pad at home that I like to draw in occasionally. I suppose this has something to do with my dad, but it's something I've never thought about too much.

"Why do you want to take art with all those weirdos?" Jordan asked me during class registration a few weeks ago.

"I don't know," I said, which was basically true. "I guess it's mostly because I'm not into the other elective options."

"Why don't you take speech?" she asked.

I rolled my eyes. "Yeah, sure. Like I want to stand up in front of everyone and *talk*."

"It'd be good for you." She poked me in the ribs with her elbow. "You know what they say: You need to face your fears head on."

She might've been right about that, but I am not and never have been a head-on kind of girl. Besides that, I am just not into public humiliation. As a result, I signed up for art.

So now, having reached the conclusion that I really do enjoy art, I've decided I'd better keep this news to myself, at least for the time being. I doubt that Jordan would get it. And once again I am surprised when I hear the end-of-class buzzer and realize that I'm still not done with the pencil sketch.

"You can stay during lunchtime to finish it," says Amy Weatherspoon as she bends over to examine my work. I glance up at her. Now Amy's really into goth, which I thought went out of style ages ago. But Amy's hair is dyed jet-black, and she wears nothing but black, paints her nails black, and has thick lines of black around her eyes, which makes her look slightly like an anemic raccoon. The only thing that isn't black is the silver safety pin that goes through the right side of her lower lip. I wonder if she did that herself.

I am already putting my pencils and stuff away and thinking about joining Jordan and her friends for lunch. "That's okay," I tell Amy, "I'll finish my sketch later."

She nods. "It's pretty good, you know."

I am totally surprised by this unexpected compliment. For some reason I didn't think Amy was the kind of girl to say anything nice.

"Thanks," I tell her without looking up. I want to say that her praise actually means something to me, since I've noticed how gifted she is in art, but the truth is, her dark appearance is fairly intimidating. Besides that, I've been out of the habit of functioning in a normal conversational manner.

"You staying during lunch, Amy?" calls Edgar Peebles. Now this is the kind of guy who actually lends credibility to Jordan's "art geek" theory. I mean, he wears the same light-blue sweatshirt almost every day, and his thick, red hair looks like someone covered it with a bowl before cutting it. But at least he's kind to everyone, even the kids who are anything *but* to him. This is the first year I've seen him around school, and although he seems younger than me, I think I heard someone say that he's a junior.

"Yeah, I wanna work on my pen and ink," says Amy as she returns to her corner by the window.

Amy's pen and ink is a grotesque rendition of a "rock" wall that is mainly constructed from skulls and bones and small dead animals. Not really my thing, but I can tell her drawing skills are far superior to mine—and everyone else in art class for that matter.

"See ya," calls Amy as I shoulder my backpack and head for the door.

"Yeah," I call back. "Later."

I try not to think too much about Jordan's new friends as I head for the cafeteria. I remind myself of the things that Jordan suggested I do. Smile more, laugh at their jokes, be nice. *I can do that,* I tell myself as I pick up a sticky tray and get in line. Today I make sure to choose food that is (1) easy to eat, (2) not likely to spill, and (3) looks like something Jordan's new friends might eat. Passing up the tacos, which look messy though tempting, I go for a tossed green salad and wheat roll. It seems fairly safe. I pay for my food and proceed to "the" table. I can feel my chest tighten and my heart beginning to race as I remember the last time I sat there and drenched my best friend in the remnants of my lunch.

"Hey, Kara," calls Jordan, "come sit here."

I smile at her, thankful that she actually extended an audible invitation. I am not ready to just walk right on over there and sit down. The cheerleaders are wearing their new uniforms today. That alone makes their table look like the elite club, although a few other girls are dressed in civilian clothes. But mostly the table looks like a small sea of red and blue.

"Thanks," I say, instantly questioning whether I should've said that or not. It's not like I want to appear too needy—or nerdy—as it would seem.

"I like your sweater, Kara," says Jordan as I sit down in the empty space across from her, right next to Ashley Crow, who is thick into conversation with Amber Elliot.

I try not to register surprise at Jordan's comment, since we both know she's the one who picked out this particular sweater in the first place. "Thanks," I say in what I hope sounds like a casual voice. I pick up my fork and stab a piece of lettuce.

"Yeah, it's cool," says Shawna. "Where'd you get it anyway?"

"The Gap," I answer, quickly remembering to smile before I take a bite.

The conversation moves swiftly to clothes and I am, fortunately, able to simply nod and smile and act like I'm completely enthralled with their opinions on fashion, which basically amount to a what's-hot-and-what's-not discussion.

"Did you see what Megan Erickson has on today?" asks Betsy Mosler. She makes this horrified face. "It's this awful pink number. She looks just like a Power Puff Girl."

This makes everyone laugh. And, like a puppet, I laugh right along with them. Yet, at the same time, I feel slightly bad for Megan.

"How about Goth Girl," says Amber Elliot.

"Who's that?" asks Jordan, looking around the cafeteria for the next victim.

"Oh, she's not here," says Amber. "Goth Girl may not have any fashion sense, but at least she has the sense to lay low."

"She's talking about Amy Weatherspoon," Shawna explains to

Jordan, who's still looking slightly confused. "Now talk about your fashion disaster. That girl dresses like every day is Halloween."

Everyone laughs like they're reading the audience cue cards on the Letterman show, and despite the fact that Amy Weatherspoon just said something kind to me, I laugh too—feeling like a complete hypocrite as I do. Still, I realize that if I *don't* laugh, these girls might very well target me as the brunt of their next fashion joke. In fact, as I watch the girls interacting with each other and virtually ignoring me, I realize that I probably already have been. Often, I'm sure.

I'm certain that the cafeteria clock has stopped now, because lunchtime is running twice as long as it normally would, but I am determined not to be the first one to leave this table of red and blue. I feel fairly certain that such a move would only invite open season on me. And so I smile and nod and laugh when appropriate and just stay put. I manage to eat about half of my salad, but my stomach is feeling more and more like it's tying itself into tight little knots.

"Have you guys heard the latest?" asks Amber suddenly. The tone of her voice says this is breaking news and the entire table becomes instantly hushed. "Clarise Owens just told me that Brett Hawkins asked Gwen Morris out."

"You're kidding!" declares Betsy as if this must be illegal, immoral, or just plain ignorant. "Brett is really taking her out?"

Amber nods. "It's true. Ask Clarise."

"You're just jealous, Betsy," teases Ashley.

"No way!" says Betsy. "I am *not* jealous of Gwen Morris. Everyone knows she's a fat, ugly cow."

"Apparently Brett doesn't think so," says Amber.

"Yeah," says Ashley as she squares off her shoulders and sits a bit straighter. It looks like she's trying to show off her overly large chest. As if she needs to. "Some guys like a woman with curves."

"Yeah," says Betsy. "*You* should know."

Ashley narrows her eyes now. "Are you calling *me* a cow?"

Thankfully, the lunch bell finally rings and the table begins to clear, although Ashley and Betsy are still going at each other. I have to wonder about this as I dump my tray. I mean, if these girls are that hard on each other, how tough might they be on an outsider like me?

"Now that wasn't so bad, was it?" asks Jordan as she catches up with me.

I shrug. "I guess not."

She smiles. "You did great, Kara. Just keep it up and everything will be cool."

I don't mention to her that it feels like I'm getting a serious stomach ulcer or high blood pressure or that I'm freaked that my antiperspirant has probably failed me today.

"You coming to the game tonight?" she asks as she adjusts the skin-tight top of her blue and red uniform. "It's our first one, you know. And then there's the dance afterward too."

Normally Jordan and I would always go to games and dances together—when we went, anyway, which wasn't always. "I don't know," I say.

She stops right in the middle of the hallway and just stares at me like I'm totally losing it. "You *have* to come to our game tonight, Kara. You're my *best* friend and this is my first night to cheer. I can't believe you'd considering ditching me like that."

I force a goofy grin. "Hey, I'm just kidding, Jordan. Of course I plan to come."

She smiles now. "Well, that's better. Sheesh, you were really starting to worry me."

"Sorry."

"I'd offer you a ride," she says lightly, "but the cheerleaders are supposed to get there early to set some things up."

"That's okay."

"But my parents are going to be there. Of course, they'll be sitting in the general admission section, but I'm sure you could sit with them if you want."

So now I am wondering how I can possibly manage to pack up the nerve to go to a football game by myself. I mean it's nice to think I could sit with the Fergusons, which would beat sitting all alone. But isn't it kind of lame to sit in the adult section? But if I don't, who will I talk to? I am not good at this *independent* thing. I even consider inviting my little sister to come along with me just so I won't have to sit by myself. Now tell me, how pathetic is that?

six

I DO NOT KNOW WHY I WASTED MY TIME COMING TO THIS STUPID FOOT-ball game. First of all, it's freezing cold out here, and besides that our team totally sucks — it's forty-five to three in the second half. But the icing on the cake is that Jordan has completely ignored me.

I thought she might come over and say hi at halftime. But no. She didn't so much as wave to me. I feel like a complete idiot coming to a moronic football game just to watch my "best" friend (or not) cheerleading. What in the world is wrong with me? And even when I searched the general-admission crowd until I finally spotted her parents, it was plain to see that they were having a great time with several other couples. I would definitely not fit in.

And so I decide to leave at the beginning of the fourth quarter. My hands and feet are numb with cold, and no one has said more than two words to me all night long. I think there is nothing as lonely as being alone in a crowd. And I know that I cannot take it for another minute. I invited Bree to come with me, but she had plans to go to a slumber party. I considered asking Mom, just so I could have an excuse to sit in the general admission section and possibly hang out with Jordan's family, but Mom had already made plans to go out with friends. As I walk down the stadium steps and across the parking lot, I cannot help but think I am a pathetic loser.

I notice what appear to be Amy Weatherspoon and some of her weird friends. They are hanging like dark shadows on the perimeter of the parking lot, huddled together around a bench, and I can see a circle of cigarette—or perhaps it's grass—smoke rising above them like a halo or perhaps smoke from a campfire. I wonder why they even came here tonight since none of them appear to be serious football fans. Then I realize that they probably plan to go to the dance afterward. And at least they don't have to walk in by themselves.

Fortunately (or not, depending on how you look at it), it only takes a few minutes for me to get home. I unlock the deadbolt on the door and let myself in, eager to get warm again, although our apartment is cold since Mom always turns the thermostat down when we're not home. I make instant cocoa in the microwave, telling myself that perhaps if I can just get warm and regain some confidence, then perhaps I can somehow manage to make myself go back to school in time for the dance. Or not. I'm still not sure. I sip my cocoa in the silent, semidark apartment, feeling (I hate to admit) extremely sorry for myself.

It seems like everyone on the planet has a life and friends, everyone except for me, that is. I sit on the stone sofa and look out the front window. I can barely see the school, or rather the lights in the parking lot, from here. I notice a few cars beginning to leave now and figure the game must be over. Some people, like parents, will be going home to call it a night. But others, like Jordan and her cheerleading friends, will be dashing out to get something to eat, or perhaps to change from their uniforms into something "cooler" to wear to the dance. Others, who don't have access to cars, will just hang out in the parking lot, visiting with friends and snarfing down the bargain hot dogs left over from the game, before they head over to the cafeteria, unfashionably early, for the dance.

What is wrong with me anyway? Why am I sitting up here in the dark all by myself on a Friday night? When did I become such a hopeless loser anyway? Or was I simply like this all along but didn't even notice? Perhaps I've never been anything more than Jordan Ferguson's shadow. But maybe I don't care either. After all, it *was* a good life. Everything was a lot more fun when Jordan was around, and so much easier too. Is this all my fault? Do I just need to try harder? Take control of my life?

I can just imagine Jordan saying, "Get off your rear, Kara Hendricks! And get yourself on over to the dance right this minute!"

Instead, I meticulously fix myself a peanut butter and jelly sandwich. I take time to make it just the way I like, even trimming off the crusts. Then I pour myself a tall glass of milk and stand over the kitchen sink and quietly consume my little feast.

I go to the bathroom now and stare at myself in the mirror. I took some extra time before the game to really fix myself up. And to my surprise, I still don't look half bad.

"There are lots of kids who are way worse looking than you," I tell the sad-eyed image in the mirror. "But they're not afraid to get out there and have a good time." I lean forward and scowl at my reflection. "What is your problem anyway?"

And so, amazingly, my little motivational speech works, and I find myself marching back over to the school. I pay my three bucks and walk boldly into the dance where I am surprised to discover that although the music is booming, there aren't very many kids there yet. It seems I am one of the losers who showed up unfashionably early, and Jordan and her friends are nowhere in sight. Even so, I go and get a soda and find a chair in a dark corner. If you have to be a wallflower, it's best to do it as inconspicuously as possible. But at least I have a clear view of the door from where I'm sitting, and I figure I can head straight for Jordan when she gets here. I even decide to use this time to design the perfect greeting.

"Hey, Jordan," I will coolly say. "I just got here too. I had to leave the game early, but you did really great tonight." I know how Jordan likes compliments, and I figure that my praise should ingratiate me to her.

But after waiting and waiting, I wonder if she and her friends even plan on coming. I know it seems stupid, but I feel like I've been stood up. Finally, I can take it no longer. I stand up and head for the door. Fortunately no one seems to notice me. Not that they ever have. And I wonder why I even care.

I hurry through the darkness and fog toward our apartment complex. I try not to imagine where Jordan and her new friends are hanging tonight. I don't want to spend any more time thinking about her than she does thinking about me. I feel certain that Jordan and I are truly history now, and I wonder why I even bothered to make myself believe otherwise. I can really be a complete fool sometimes.

The apartment is quiet and dark and cold when I get home. I don't even bother to turn on the lights or heat. And, relieved that my mom isn't there to ask how my evening went, I retreat to my room and lay down on my bed with my clothes still on. I lay there in the darkness and try not to cry. It feels as if someone has placed a bag of heavy rocks upon my chest. It's hard to breathe, hard to think, hard to live.

Part of me feels pretty stupid, fairly ridiculous, and even slightly neurotic for caring this much. And I wonder why I am acting like such a total nerd? But another part of me is dark blue, and I feel buried alive in a deep and bitter grief. I am certain my life is over.

seven

WHAT DO YOU DO ALL WEEKEND WHEN YOU DON'T HAVE A FRIEND TO hang with? Thanks to going to bed early on Friday night, I wake up earlier than usual the next day. The apartment is quiet and still. I figure my mom is sleeping in, and Bree is probably still sacked out at the slumber party. It's times like this when I wish I had a dog, or even a cat. Of course, pets aren't allowed at our apartment complex.

For years Mom has been saying we're going to move into a "real" house, but it never seems to happen. This is probably my dad's fault, since he's about ten years delinquent on his child-support payments. Mom says if he ever gets caught he'll probably go to prison for a long time. Sometimes I feel sorry for him, but not today. Today I think it's his fault that my life is such a mess. I'm not exactly sure what brings me to this particular conclusion, but somehow it makes sense.

I fix myself a bowl of granola cereal and mechanically shovel it down without actually tasting it. I rinse my bowl in the sink then glance up at the kitchen clock to see that it's only 7:32. Already I am asking myself if I should call Jordan today. I rehearse in my head what I might say to her. I would casually ask why she didn't show at the dance last night. And when she answers I would just act like, "Hey, that's cool. No big deal." And then she would invite me to come over and hang with her. Maybe we'd go see that new movie that she's been waiting to see.

But I know that I'm not really going to call her today. And I seriously doubt that she will call me. I'm not even sure why I know this. I guess I can just feel it in my bones.

I throw on my sweats and lace up my running shoes. Jordan was the one who got me into jogging. She did it to keep her weight down. I did it just to be with her. But I haven't jogged in weeks and I think maybe I need to today. Maybe it will help eject me out of this funk. Then, as I'm about to go out the door, I decide to do something different. I slip a sketch pad and some pencils into an old backpack, then put it on and take off.

I jog at a pretty good pace for about thirty minutes, but by then I'm out of breath and developing a side ache. I should've known I was out of shape and taken it easier. But maybe I don't care. In some ways I think this physical pain is much easier to deal with than the ache that's going on inside of me. I stop running when I reach the park. Rubbing my side, I simply walk. Other joggers run past me, usually in pairs. I remember how Jordan and I used to meet here and run together. But shortly before school started she told me jogging wasn't her favorite type of exercise. She'd started working out on her mom's treadmill in front of the TV. I might've opted for something like that too, if it were an option. Or not. There is something calming about having the sky overhead.

As I walk through the park, it occurs to me that I really don't know who I am anymore. I wonder if I ever did. I wonder if I have always been living in Jordan's shadow, making the choices that I hoped would please her, altering myself to fit in better with her life and to compliment her personality. When she bubbled, I watched. When she talked, I listened. When she told me to jump, I asked how high. Suddenly I wonder if I have a personality of my own at all. I wonder if I even exist or am simply something that Jordan Ferguson conjured up—like an imaginary playmate that she no longer needs. I see a squashed soda can in the grass beside the foot path, and I know how it must feel. Used up and discarded. I pick it up and toss it into the trash can.

I stop walking when I reach the duck pond and sit down on a damp cement bench. I can feel the cold wetness soaking through my sweats, but I don't really care. I remember how Jordan and I used to come here as kids. We always brought a few pieces of stale bread to feed the ducks. A couple of curious ducks approach me now, probably thinking I have something for them. But I do not. I don't have anything for anyone—not even for myself.

I feel that familiar lump growing in my throat again and I'm afraid I'm going to cry, but I'm determined not to. Crying won't change anything. All it does is make my eyes puffy.

I gaze out on the pond and tell myself it's a pretty sight that I should attempt to enjoy. Then I remember that I brought along my sketch pad. I remove my backpack and pull out the pad, opening it up to reveal a clean white page. I take out a pencil and chew on its eraser as I look out over the scene before me. Three tall evergreen trees cut into the cloudy sky on the far side of the pond. Several ducks move gracefully over the glassy surface of the water.

I stare at the drawing paper for several minutes. I imagine myself hunched over as I intently sketch the general outline. Then I would fill it in, giving the picture details and textures and shadows and light. But I just sit there and do nothing but stare at the blank piece of paper. It's like a self-portrait of my life. Empty and flat and bleak. And I don't even know where to begin to make it into anything else. I close the pad, shove it into my backpack, and stand.

With a lump in my throat, I begin walking toward home. I think maybe I will go back to bed. But by the time I reach the apartment complex I am already hoping that Jordan has unexpectedly dropped by. She's been known to do that sometimes. I imagine her and my mom sitting at the breakfast bar drinking a cup of freshly brewed coffee. I dash up the stairs and open the door to see the apartment is still quiet, just the way I left it. I glance at the clock to see it's barely past nine, and I feel lost to think of all the time that is left in this day. It's like a desert of loneliness stretching out for miles and miles.

Then, with the tiniest spark of hope, I go over to check our answering machine. It's entirely possible that Jordan called while I was out, and that she might be, right this very minute, cooking up some fantastic plan for our day. But the little red light is not blinking. Like me, it is dark and blank.

I take a long shower and, after I wash my hair, I realize I am out of conditioner. I shake and squeeze the stubborn bottle but can barely get a drop out of it. It's a special kind of salon conditioner, with aloe and avocado, which Jordan's sister Abbie insists is perfect for my kind of hair. But like everything else in my life, it's bailed on me as well. I finally give up and toss the stupid thing onto the floor. But at least I have something to do now. As I towel dry I decide I must go to the mall to get some more. A feeble excuse for an outing, perhaps, but it's all I have at the moment.

I take great care to dress, putting on my best jeans and my second-favorite top, a hooded sweatshirt with what I hope is still a fairly cool logo. You never know when something will go out of style on you. According to Jordan, one day it's hot and the next day it's not. I've never been very good at figuring these things out for myself, and I'm pretty certain that I am about to become Jackson High's next fashion disaster now that Jordan's influence is evaporating from my life.

I take more care than usual with my makeup too. Not that I use much, because I don't. But I make sure that my lip gloss is on evenly. And I even apply mascara, remembering how Abbie says that everyone should wear it. I give myself a final inspection and decide that it will have to do. Of course, I won't consciously acknowledge why I am going to such trouble just to go pick up a bottle of hair conditioner. But the truth is, I'm seriously hoping to run into Jordan at the mall. I know it's totally pathetic, but I cannot seem to help myself.

"Where're you going?" asks my mom from her usual Saturday spot. She's curled up on the leather couch by the window, looking out of context in her fuzzy blue bathrobe, a mug of coffee in one hand, and the partially read newspaper spread out all over her lap.

"The mall," I answer.

"Meeting Jordan there?"

I shrug. "Maybe." I can feel my mom studying me now, and all I want to do is get out of there before she says something upsetting.

"Everything okay, Kara?"

"I guess so."

"Bree thinks that you and Jordan had a fight or something."

"We *didn't* have a fight." I can hear the sharp edge of exasperation in my voice now. But I'm irritated that my mom thinks she can get accurate information about *my* life from Bree. If she wanted to know about *my* life, why didn't she just come straight to *me?* Okay, maybe I'm being a little unreasonable.

"Well, I haven't seen Jordan around here much lately." My mom sets her coffee mug down on the side table with a thud. "So, how does she like cheerleading? Wasn't last night the first game?"

I can tell this is a trick question. She's trying to reel me in and find out what's going on. This might've worked a few days ago, but

I don't really want to talk about it now. "Jordan likes cheerleading just fine."

"So, what do you think about it?"

"Cheerleading?" I try to look confused. "Oh, I guess it's okay if that's what you want to do."

"That's not what I meant, Kara. I mean, how is it affecting your friendship with Jordan? Is it hard on you watching your best friend do something you're not involved in?"

It's times like this when I wish my mom didn't read Oprah's magazine from cover to cover. It's like she keeps trying to play junior psychiatrist with Bree and me. I wish she'd just give it up, or else just get real and *talk* about things instead of trying to find solutions for everything.

"Jordan has done lots of things that I'm not involved in," I remind my mom. "Like she's done debate team and gymnastics . . . " I try to think of something else but come up empty.

"So, everything's okay with you two girls then?" My mom is frowning like she's still pretty skeptical.

"Everything's fine."

Now she smiles. "Well, you know you can talk to me, Kara. If you need to."

I nod. "Thanks, Mom. I know I can." And it's weird, but I almost wish I hadn't blown her off just then. Maybe I *can* talk to her. But now it's too late.

"Have fun."

So I head out the door with those two words ringing in my brain. *Have fun. Have fun. Have fun.* Yeah, sure!

By the time I reach the bus stop I'm thinking maybe this is a stupid idea. Maybe I'm just setting myself up for another big disappointment. But then, I really do need some conditioner.

By the time the bus pulls over at the mall, I am feeling much more positive about my day. I'm thinking I'll probably run into Jordan for sure, and we'll get some lunch together. Maybe sushi, since that's been Jordan's favorite lately. And we'll laugh and talk, and everything will be just like old times.

It's a little past noon when I go to the shop that carries my conditioner. I want to take care of my little "errand" first so that it will be obvious by my shopping bag that I had an actual reason to come to the mall. I mean I don't want it to look like I'm just hanging out here, hoping I'll run into Jordan. How pathetic is that? No, I came for honest-to-goodness shopping purposes.

"Can I help you?"

The voice is familiar, and I turn around and am shocked to see Ashley Crow standing behind the counter.

"You work here?"

She shrugs. "Yeah. My mom bought this shop last month and she's been making me work here on Saturdays."

"Well, at least it should save you some money on hair products and stuff."

"Yeah. It is pretty cool to be able to just grab what you want when you need it."

I tell her what I came for and then she asks me if I've tried this new conditioner.

"I think it would be great for your hair, Kara."

"Really? I kind of liked the other one."

"Yeah. It's a really good conditioner too, but did you know that you're supposed to alternate brands so that you don't get buildup?"

I study her for a moment, wondering if this is some kind of a setup. Like, would I use this stuff and end up with hair that hangs like pond slime?

"Look, Kara, trust me, this stuff is good." She opens the bottle and holds it out. "Smell it."

"Hmmm, that is nice."

"It's what I use myself."

I look at her hair, which is a nice dark shade of auburn and similar to mine in texture, and I decide to trust her.

"Thanks, Ashley," I say as she gives me my change.

Then she leans forward and speaks to me in what seems a fairly confidential tone. "I know we can seem like a pretty tough crowd sometimes, Kara. But once you get used to us, we're not so bad. You just have to hang in there is all."

I feel encouraged as I leave the shop. On one hand I can hardly believe that Ashley Crow has been friendly to me, but at the same time I'm worried that there might be a trick too. Like maybe there really is something wrong with that conditioner. But I tell myself to quit being so paranoid. And, with my purple plastic bag in hand, I proceed down the mall, stopping at Jordan's favorite shops and glancing all around as I walk past racks and shelves. But I'm not looking at the clothes, or even at the shoes, which everyone knows is my particular shopping weakness. Instead, I am searching the aisles for a certain petite someone with blonde hair.

Finally, I give up on the shops and head over to the eating area. Perhaps she's already in line at the Sushi Bar. But she's not. I consider standing in line myself, hoping that Jordan will come and discover me here already. She'll laugh and say, "Can you believe it? We both wanted sushi at the same time!"

"Can I help you?" asks an Asian girl with lime-green hair from behind the counter.

Embarrassed to be standing in line for no good reason, I go ahead and place an order for the kind of sushi that Jordan usually gets, along with hot tea. I wait while the girl puts four tight little rice-and-seaweed rolls on a paper plate. Then I try not to look too obvious as I glance over my shoulder, but I don't see Jordan anywhere.

I pay for the sushi and go to a table where I'll have a good view of anyone who comes or goes from the Sushi Bar. I take my time eating my sushi, which isn't hard since I don't think I really like sushi anyway. By the time I finish my tea, which tastes a bit like seaweed too, it's cold. I feel like an idiot as I dump the garbage from my tray. I wonder if I am losing my mind as I head back across the mall and toward the bus stop. What was I thinking? Really! That I would just magically bump into Jordan and everything would be just peachy? *Get real, Kara!*

I stand at the bus stop without really seeing anyone or anything. I just want out of this place. I want to go home. And maybe I really will go back to bed this time!

"Kara!"

Surprised to hear my name, and thinking I may have imagined it, I look up to see a red car full of girls. It's slowing down by the bus stop, and now I see that Amber Elliott is at the wheel and Jordan is waving from an open window in the back seat.

"You on your way home?" she calls.

I hold up my stupid purple plastic bag and nod mutely.

"See ya!" She waves wildly as the car makes a fast left turn. I can hear squeals of laughter coming from the fast-moving car as they disappear in pursuit of a vacant parking place.

Then the big bus pulls up with its hissing brakes and the stench of diesel exhaust, and I am swallowed into its gritty, stuffy interior. I sit close to the front and stare blankly out the smeared window, wishing I were someone else.

eight

"LEAVE ME ALONE!" I SHOUT AT BREE AS I ATTEMPT TO PUSH HER OUT OF my bedroom and close the door. I can't believe she just walked right in here like she owns the place!

"Man!" Bree leaves her foot in the doorway and stares at me as if I'm a three-headed monster. "You are such a total grump, Kara! I only wanted to borrow your—"

"Look!" I yell over the music that's playing pretty loudly on my CD player. "Whatever it is you want, I am *not* loaning it to you! *Get it?*"

"Fine!" She's glaring at me now. "But don't come begging me for—"

I push back her foot and slam my door midsentence. My sister is such an idiot! As if I have *ever* "begged" her for anything. Well, except to be left alone right now. She is such a total pest.

I flop back down on my bed and experience the tiniest twinge of guilt for being so mean to her. But the feeling is short-lived and quickly replaced with this fierce red-hot anger that seems to be filling my entire being this evening. I honestly feel as if I hate everyone on the planet right now. They all make me sick. But most of all I despise Jordan Ferguson. I don't know why I ever thought she was my friend. I'm sure that if I turned on the six o'clock news and learned that she'd been run over by a freight train, I'd just throw back my head and laugh. Okay, maybe not. But it *feels* like I would.

Mom wanted me to go have Sunday brunch with her and Bree this morning, but I flat-out refused. For one thing, the idea of eating a bunch of soggy buffet food makes me want to hurl, but beyond that I cannot imagine sitting in a padded booth with my mom and sister and acting like everything is just peachy. Because the fact is, my life totally sucks!

Now I am wondering if there's any way I can get out of going to school tomorrow. Mom is already starting to think I'm "coming down with something." Maybe I should just run with that. I know I feel sick. My stomach hurts and my head is throbbing. Now that I think about it, I feel like I might even be running a fever.

Of course, I also feel extremely angry. I don't ever recall feeling quite this mad about anything before. But I am furious. It's like I've had all this time these past couple of days to really figure everything all out. Suddenly, it's plain to see that I've been the biggest fool ever. I realize now that Jordan has done nothing but use me all these years when she pretended to be my friend.

I can't believe how easily duped I was. It's almost funny to think of how I was such a "handy" friend for her too. I mean how stupid is that? But there I was, *always* available. *Always* adoring. *Always* willing to go along with whatever totally lame idea she came up with next. Well, *almost* always. I guess I didn't fall for the debate thing or cheerleading tryouts. Although I did go out for the balance beam in gymnastics, but I twisted my ankle at the first practice so that was that. Still, it seems crystal clear to me that I have played her insignificant pawn for a long, long time.

It reminds me of those silly women who keep those goofy-looking lap dogs. They lead them around on rhinestone leashes like little four-legged shadows. That's how I see myself. I was Jordan's doting little dog, but the really pathetic part was she didn't even need a leash for me. I followed her willingly!

Naturally, this whole thing just totally makes me sick now. I think, man, how pitifully desperate I must've appeared to everyone all this time. Just faithfully following Jordan around, coming and going at her beck and call. Well, I'll bet you that none of her cheerleading friends will be like that. It might be time for Jordan to wake up and smell the coffee! I hope she feels bad when she figures it out. I hope she realizes what she lost when she tossed me aside like a worn-out pair of sneakers. I hope she regrets this until the day she dies.

Because I have decided that no matter what Jordan does or says next, I will *not*, I repeat *not*, consider her my best friend ever again. I will not fall for her tricks and deceptions. I will not be duped again. I'm not even sure I can consider her a casual friend anymore. Not after this.

I sneaked a peek at one of Mom's Oprah magazines in the bathroom this afternoon. They're not so bad really. In fact, I found an article about friends today, and I can see now that Jordan didn't have one single quality a person would look for in a lasting friendship. But it makes me wonder why I was so pitifully desperate to hang on to her like that. Why did I think that Jordan Ferguson was the best I could do?

Here's the truth of it: Jordan has brainwashed me over the years. I think she's like one of those weird cult leaders, like that Jones guy in South America that we read about in humanities class. He somehow managed to make his followers believe everything he said. Like he was a prophet or God or something. I think that's what Jordan did to me. It's like I quit thinking for myself. Like when I met her I just handed over my brain and said, "Go ahead and do what you like with it." Sheesh, I make myself sick!

But then I have to ask, what kind of a twisted person would knowingly do that to someone else? What kind of friend would manipulate you for her own personal benefit? It's scary if you think about it. I guess I should be thankful I got away when I did.

Still, I don't feel the least bit thankful. I just feel mad, furious, outraged. And I can imagine myself telling Jordan off too. I can just hear myself saying, "Jordan Ferguson, you are such an egomaniac! You are selfish and shallow and narcissistic and vain! I don't know how I ever believed you were my friend. But I am so glad that I figured it out. I hope you and your new friends are happy together, because I'm sure you all totally deserve each other!" And then I will turn on my heel and just storm off. Ah, that would be such a good feeling.

However, I doubt that I'll be able to pull it off. So I will have to console myself with my petty little vengeance daydreams. I have several of them now. One of my favorites is set at a pep assembly. I think we're actually supposed to have one next week. Anyway, I imagine the cheerleaders doing one of those pyramids. Naturally, Jordan, little sprite that she is, will be on top, but as soon as she climbs up there her pyramid will collapse and she will fall flat on her face, maybe even break her cute little nose. Then Amber will stand up and say, in a very loud voice, "Been putting on a little weight, have you, Ferguson?" And the whole school will laugh.

Another one has Jordan walking down the hall at school and she drops a book. She bends over to pick it up and her jeans are so tight that they just split wide open right down the middle, totally exposing her rear end. And she is wearing these ugly granny panties and everyone just stares at her in horror then laughs.

Okay, I do feel a teeny bit of guilt when I harbor such horrendously mean thoughts toward my ex-best friend. But then I simply remind myself, she deserves it!

Before I go to bed I drop hints that I'm not feeling too well. "I think I'm getting a bug or something," I tell my mom as I make myself a cup of ginger-chamomile tea. (Mom is always trying to get us to drink this awful stuff when we're sick.)

She puts a hand on my forehead. "You don't feel like you're running a fever."

"She's got grouchitis," says Bree, making a face behind Mom's back.

"Sometimes people get grouchy when they're sick," offers my mom.

I take a sip of tea and attempt to look pitiful.

"What is it that's bothering you?" asks Mom.

"My stomach and my head. I think I'm getting the flu."

She frowns. "It seems a little early for flu season, but I suppose . . . "

"She's just mad that Jordan dumped her," says Bree in a taunting tone.

"Shut up!" I glare at her, controlling myself from wanting to reach out and really smack my smart-mouthed little sister.

"We don't say 'shut up,'" my mom reminds me.

"Well, I wish she would bug off then."

"Bree, why don't you go to your room so Kara and I can talk."

"Yeah, fine, send *me* to my room," whines Bree. "Like *I'm* the problem here. Well, at least *I* have friends!"

"Bree!" I hear the warning in Mom's voice, then Bree's door slams behind her.

I squirt some honey into my tea, stir it, then take another sip.

Mom sits down at a stool by the counter. "What's the problem, Kara?"

"The problem is that I feel like crud, Mom." I say this with all the emphasis I can muster, then set my mug down loudly on the countertop and look at her, hoping I look pretty sick.

"But I can tell that something else is going on, Kara. I'm guessing Bree is right. Does this have something to do with Jordan?"

I make a dramatic groaning sound. "Why do you have to keep thinking everything is about Jordan? Sheesh! Yeah, we used to be friends, but we're not anymore. It's no big deal, Mom. Get over it."

She frowns. "I'm not the one making it a problem."

I hold up my hands. "Well, neither am I. I'm just telling you I feel kind of sick. You're the one blowing everything out of proportion here." I know this is a good tactic to distract my mom. I throw whatever it is right back in her face and often it can really confuse things.

"I'm not blowing anything out of proportion, Kara. I'm just trying to figure this out with you."

I pick up my tea mug and start to walk away now. "The only thing wrong with me is that I feel sick. *Sorry!* I guess no one's allowed to be sick in this place."

"That's not it—"

"Well, I don't know what 'it' is then. But I am going to bed. Goodnight, *Mother.*" We both know that I only call her "Mother" when I'm mad. And I'm mad now. Following my little sister's example, I too slam my door. Only louder. I feel just slightly sorry for my mom. I know this isn't her fault. But at the same time I don't know what makes her think she can fix anything. All I wanted was a little sympathy and permission to stay home tomorrow. Of course, I realize, my mom can't actually make me go to school if I don't want to. *And I don't want to.*

I stay up really late. It's not like I'm doing much of anything, just quietly listening to my Alanis Morissette CD. Jordan can't stand Alanis, she says all she does is complain, but I happen to like her and relate to her lyrics. Ironically enough, I am also flipping through a stupid *Cosmo* magazine that Jordan left the last time she spent the night, which must've been in August shortly before school started. Finally I open the window and close my heating vents, allowing my room to fill with cold air. Then I actually take off my pajamas and lay on my bed until I am shivering. I am thinking perhaps I can catch a cold. I know that colds are really a result of germs, but I've also heard that if you get run down or chilled or whatever, you can wear down your resistance to germs and then get sick. That's what I'm hoping for—either a cold, or if I'm lucky, pneumonia. It would be so perfect if I were to get pneumonia and have to be hospitalized.

I wonder if Jordan would come to visit me in the hospital. I can imagine her coming into my room with a big bouquet of flowers and balloons, maybe even a stuffed rabbit (since she knows how I love bunnies), and she would stand next to my bed and plead and beg for my forgiveness. But I would just turn my head away from her without speaking. Perhaps I might even breathe my last breath while she was standing there. But I wouldn't forgive her. No way! I would make her suffer for the rest of her life for hurting me like this.

My teeth are chattering like castanets now and I wonder how much longer I can take this form of freezing torture. But then I realize it's also a pretty good distraction to the cruddy way I feel inside. Maybe it's worth it. Now, if only I can wake up half dead!

nine

NO SUCH LUCK. I WAKE UP FEELING PERFECTLY FINE. WELL, AT LEAST physically. I still feel rotten on the inside.

"How are you feeling today?" my mom asks after she cracks open my bedroom door and peeks in.

I am still in bed, tired from staying up so late. "Awful," I mutter, making my best attempt at looking sick.

She comes into my room and touches my forehead again. I do not understand what makes mothers think they are walking-talking thermometers. But I think somewhere during the process of giving birth and changing diapers, they actually begin to believe they have this supernatural sense.

"You feel normal to me, honey." She pushes some hair off my forehead and smiles. "But I can make you an appointment with Dr. Peterson if you like."

Okay, I'm not dumb. Despite that warm motherly smile, I know this is a threat. I absolutely hate going to the doctor. I hate it when I'm sick and even more so when I'm not.

"Fine," I growl. "I'll *go* to school, but if I spread some really horrible disease to everyone, they will all have you to thank."

"Well, I've got to run, Kara. I'm already a little late. Have a good day."

Have a good day! Yeah, you bet. I grumble all the way to the bathroom. Thankfully, Bree is done now, but she's left her usual trail of wet towels and shower debris all over the place. I kick them out of my way and growl as I turn on the water. Why is life so unfair?

I realize I'll have to hurry if I don't want to be late. And despite my foul mood I don't really want to be late. I'm not particularly fond of that kind of attention. And so I quickly dress, snatch up my backpack, and dash to school with still-wet hair. Why should I care?

Naturally, I see Jordan (or rather she sees me) in the hallway. Of course, she looks perfect with every hair in place, and wearing what looks like a new outfit. Probably a little something she picked up with her new friends at the mall the other day.

"Are you okay, Kara?" She frowns slightly as she peers at me and I wonder why she can't manage to come up with something new to ask me. But I feel too much like a sideshow freak to mention this, and besides, I can see some of her friends now eyeing me curiously too, including Ashley Crow. She seemed so nice when I bought conditioner from her on Saturday, but now she looks at me like maybe I have head lice. Jordan shakes her head. "You don't look too—"

"*I'm fine!*" I snap at her. "Just late is all." Then I rush off toward the English department as if I have an appointment with the president. As I speed down the breezeway, I refuse to allow Jordan's fake interest in my welfare, or more likely my sorry appearance, to slow me down. I cannot afford her brand of pity or concern right now. It's just too freaking bad if I don't look cool enough to be seen with her and her new shallow friends. It's not like they want me around them anyway. What do I care?

I repeat those four words through my mind as I walk. *What do I care? What do I care? What do I care?* It reminds me of an old picture book that I used to like as a kid. It's about this little blue engine, but somehow I think I have the words all wrong. *What do I care? What do I care? Choo-choo — get outta my way!*

I make it to English just as the tardy bell rings, but it doesn't look like Mr. Parker bothered to mark me late. I slip into a sideline seat and wish I were someone else. I don't even look up when Jordan and Shawna walk in, even later than I was, but I do wonder if Mr. Parker has noticed. I keep my eyes downward, pretending to focus on our reading assignment although the words look blurry and fuzzy. I vaguely wonder if I might need glasses.

Then, like zombie-girl, I trudge through my morning classes. I cannot imagine going through day after day like this for *three whole years!* Finally, I'm in art class, and I almost feel like I can breathe again. I am able to forget other things as I find myself getting pulled into my pencil sketch. I just hope that I can finish it before lunchtime.

My subject for this sketch is from a photo I found in Ms. Clark's "inspiration" box. It's an old beater pickup that's partially covered with old vines. I'm sure it doesn't even run, but something about it intrigues me and I feel a growing connection to this abandoned and neglected truck. I'm working really hard to get the shadows around the fender just right. But I'm still not done when I hear the lunch buzzer.

"That's pretty good," says a girl's voice.

I look up to see Felicia Wong silhouetted by the sunlight coming through the window behind her. I squint to see her, curious as to whether she's serious. She steps to the side a bit so that I can see her face better, and I think she seems sincere. I've known Felicia since around fifth grade. And it's not that I expect her to be especially rude, but I used to think she was a little stuck-up or full of herself. Maybe it's because she's supposed to be so smart. Everyone says she has a genius IQ.

"Thanks," I mutter.

"Do you like art?" she asks now.

"I guess so."

"You know, some of us stay here and keep working during lunchtime," Felicia continues. "Ms. Clark doesn't mind as long as we clean up after ourselves."

"Yeah, I know."

"Oh, okay." She steps back now and her face gets this blank look, like she's trying to conceal something, and I wonder if I've offended her. Even so, I say nothing and she quickly retreats to join several kids gathered at the big table in the back of the room.

Now I feel bad and wonder why it is that I think I can act like such a jerk. I wander toward the group.

"You know," I say to Felicia, "I'd stay and draw during lunch too, but I left home in such a hurry this morning that I forgot to pack anything to eat. Plus I skipped breakfast and am feeling kind of hungry now." I know my explanation is too long and sounds lame. But it's the best I can do under the circumstances.

"I've got an apple I don't want," Felicia offers.

Now Edgar Peebles is digging through his backpack like he's hunting for hidden treasure. He pulls out a limp-looking package and holds it up hopefully. "I've got a string cheese you can have, Kara." He smiles as he adjusts his slightly crooked wire-rimmed glasses.

"Hey, it's not like I'm a poverty case," I say, probably too defensively. "I was just in a hurry, you know. Maybe I'll join you guys another time."

Felicia shakes her head like she's thinking I'm pretty weird. "Hey, no problem. Do what you like, Kara. We were just offering."

"Yeah," says Amy in a sharper tone. "We don't need anyone hanging out here who thinks she's too good for us—"

"Oh, Amy," says Felicia.

"That's not it." I narrow my eyes at Amy now.

But undeterred, she looks right back at me. "Hey, if the shoe fits—"

"Well, think whatever you like," I say in what sounds like the kind of flippant tone that I usually despise, not so very unlike the girls that Jordan's probably eating lunch with right now. "I just happen to be hungry today and I don't particularly want to eat handouts. Thanks just the same."

Then I get out of there before Amy has a chance to sling anything at me. I'm sure I offended her. I probably offended them all. But it's like I can't help it. Then I begin my little *choo-choo* rhyme again. *What do I care? What do I care?* I repeat this through my head as I chug down the hallway in search of food.

I buy my "lunch" from the big machine in the hallway. Ironically I choose an apple and some string cheese. These I quietly consume on the *other* side of the school. I am not going to chance eating on the steps by the art department. I couldn't endure the humiliation of being found there by Amy or Felicia or even that goofy old Edgar. Who names their kid *Edgar* anyway? Especially when it's followed by a name like Peebles. Some people are just nuts!

I manage to make it through my afternoon classes without running into Jordan or her stupid friends once. I am learning how to keep a *low profile*. I sit close to the doors and exit my classes as soon as the release bells ring. Then I dash, not actually running since that would draw unwanted attention, but I choose the least crowded hallway and head straight for my next class. I keep my eyes downward as I go, just in case someone tries to make eye contact. Not that anyone ever would. But this behavior helps to make me feel slightly invisible. I think I am becoming quite stealthy actually. If I can keep this up, I might someday just vanish into thin air. It wouldn't be such a bad thing really. I imagine myself like that old movie, except I would be the Invisible Girl. As soon as the final bell rings, I am heading straight for the nearest exit, ready to blow this joint for—

"Kara," calls an all-too-familiar voice.

I turn to see her, still looking like a page from one of her favorite fashion magazines. I try to form my face into an expression that I hope is a mixture of boredom and vague curiosity. But I'm afraid I look more like a deer caught in the headlights. Naturally, Jordan isn't alone. Shawna and Betsy flank her, both looking on with an air of pure disinterest. Sort of the expression I was going for, only they're actually achieving it. I'm guessing they're on their way to cheerleading practice since they've got gym bags with pom-poms hanging out of them. Subtle.

"What's going on with you?" Jordan asks me. She breaks a couple steps away from her new buddies and peers at me with that same curious expression that she'd tried on me this morning. And for whatever reason it makes me feel as if I'm going to cry. Not a good feeling.

"Nothing." I shift my backpack to my other shoulder, which is a mistake because it will only slide off and make me look even more stupid.

"Are you okay?" she persists.

"Yeah." I use a louder than necessary voice. "I'm perfectly fine, Jordan. Why shouldn't I be?" Now I stare at her, hoping I can make *her* feel uncomfortable for a change.

"I don't know. But you just seem different. I wondered if you're doing okay is all."

"Well, I just need to get home." I glance over to where Shawna and Betsy are waiting. Their expressions have switched from bored interest to tight-lipped impatience. "And it looks like you need to get to practice anyway. So don't let me keep you."

Jordan smiles now. She actually smiles! Sheesh! Just like everything is perfectly normal—just peachy keen. Makes me wanna scream.

"Okay," she says in her chirpy, cheerful, cheerleader voice. "Guess I'll see ya then."

"Yeah, later." I can hear that flat tone in my voice, but I just really don't care anymore. Why should I?

I walk home alone, the twisted little-blue-engine words running through my brain with each step. It's like I can't even stop them now. *What do I care? What do I care? What do I care?*

It isn't until I walk up the steps to the apartment that I realize I have tears running down my cheeks. I want to yell and scream at myself, to tell myself to just shape up and get over it, but instead I fall on top of my bed and just sob. I wish this could all just end.

ten

THE NEXT FEW DAYS PROCEED IN A PITIFULLY SIMILAR FASHION. I AM embarrassed to say that losing my best friend has rendered me nearly dysfunctional. I think I am totally hopeless, and it's only a matter of time before my grades begin slipping and the counselor calls and my mom suggests I go see a shrink or something. And then, well, who knows?

Jordan has pretty much quit talking to me completely now. In all fairness, this has almost as much to do with me as it does her. I pretty much blow off every attempt she makes to be *nice*. Because that's exactly how it feels to me. As if she's saying to herself, "Oh, there's that poor Kara Hendricks girl. I used to be friends with her. But now that I'm popular, I should try to be nice to her. At least for appearances' sake. I don't want anyone thinking I'm not nice." But I do my best to make it very difficult for her, and I think she's finally given up. It's somewhat of a relief to me though. I'm thinking a clean break might be the best in the long run. Less painful.

I walk through Jackson High imagining that I am invisible. I keep my eyes downcast and speak as little as possible. I'm not sure how long I can keep this up, but it seems to be working at the moment. However, I am lonely. Unspeakably lonely. And there is this dull empty ache inside of me. Sometimes I think it might actually kill me. But perhaps that would be a relief.

"I thought you said you were going to join us for lunch some-time, Kara," says Edgar Peebles as art class ends on Friday. "It's been a whole week and you haven't — "

"Don't waste your time on her," says Amy. "Kara thinks she's too good for us. She'd rather hang out with her cheerleading friends." Then she makes a pretty bad rendition of a Jackson High yell, only she substitutes some words for others with more spice.

Despite myself I have to smile. It's not something I'd want to repeat, but it is sort of funny in an off-color way. "For your informa-tion," I tell her now, "I am not friends with any of the cheerleaders."

She rolls her black-lined eyes at me. "Yeah, sure. What about you and little rally queen Jordan Ferguson?" She crosses her fingers together. "You guys are like that."

I shake my head without smiling. "Not anymore."

Amy scowls. "Don't tell me she dumped you just because she's a cheerleader?"

I shrug. "It's a mutual parting of ways."

Amy laughs in a sarcastic tone. "Yeah, that's one way to put it."

"Lighten up, Amy," says Felicia, smiling toward me now. "So, you want to join us. We already called in a pizza."

"Yeah. My treat," says Edgar. "It's a giant. Big enough for everyone."

"Half combo and half veggie," says Felicia. "You in?"

I look at the three of them and try to imagine a stranger com-bination of kids. One goth and mouthy, one weird and geeky, one smart and preppy. Go figure. "Yeah, sure," I say. "Sounds good."

So I get my stuff and bring it to the big table in back and sit down on the vacant stool next to Edgar. "What are you working on?" I ask him.

He holds up his tablet to reveal a charcoal sketch of a woman that's really quite good.

"Not bad," I say with an approving nod.

This makes him smile.

"I told Edgar that he should've done her nude," says Amy as she shakes her ink pen. "She's got a look in her eye that says she shouldn't be wearing any clothes."

This makes Edgar blush and look away.

"Ms. Clark probably wouldn't be too thrilled about that," says Felicia. "Rollin Abrams tried it last year and things got a little ugly. He ended up being excluded from the spring art fair."

"Stupid hypocrites," says Amy, shaking her head. "They expect us to be creative and open-minded, then they censor half the thoughts that come out of our heads."

"Yeah," says Felicia. "Not only that, but they make it illegal to pray in school."

"Oh, no," says Amy. "Sounds like Felicia's getting up on her religious soapbox again."

Felicia smiles in a somewhat apologetic manner. "Not really. But if you think about it, it's no different than what you're complaining about, Amy."

"How's that?" asks Amy without looking up from her pen-and-ink project.

I suddenly realize that I'm not even drawing now. I am simply sitting here, like a dummy, mesmerized by their banter. I suppose I have missed being involved in conversations. Still, I don't want to appear too desperate. So I quickly pick up my charcoal pencil and pretend to turn my attention back to my drawing. It's an old house, but I'm having a hard time getting it to look right. It seems flat and dark to me, and definitely less interesting than their conversation.

My pencil hovers as I listen.

"Well, freedom of speech shouldn't just apply to the arts," continues Felicia. "But also to religion."

"We have freedom of religion laws," says Edgar.

"Duh!" Amy looks up and scowls at him.

"But they get misinterpreted," says Felicia.

"Well, I sure don't want anyone telling me I have to *pray* in school," says Amy. "That's totally fascist."

"Right," says Felicia. "I don't think our government should tell us to pray either. But I don't think they should tell us that we can't. I also don't think they should go around stripping words that refer to God from things like the Pledge of Allegiance or songs or even our money for that matter."

"There she goes," says Amy with a big sigh. "Sorry about this, Kara. But welcome to the lunch club. We love discussing anything controversial."

Felicia laughs. "Yeah, that's probably why we wanted you to join us. You look like you might have an ax to grind."

"That's right," says Amy, pausing from her drawing to look at me with curiosity. Then she holds her pen like it's a microphone and she's the interviewer. "So, tell us, Kara Hendricks, what do *you* think of this year's Jackson High cheerleader squad?"

I make a face at her then notice Edgar is getting up to leave. "Where's he going?" I ask.

"To pick up the pizza," says Amy. "They're not allowed to deliver it on school grounds. He has to go meet them in the street."

"Oh."

I reach for my backpack and wallet. "I should probably chip in."

"Nah," says Amy. "Edgar really gets a jolt out of treating us girls to pizza. It's probably the closest thing he'll ever get to a date."

"Oh, don't be hard on him," says Felicia. "He's really sweet."

Amy leans over and looks Felicia in the eye. "Sweet enough that you'd let him take you to, say, the prom?"

Felicia shrugs. "I don't know. Maybe. I happen to have great respect for Edgar."

Amy laughs. "So do I. But you won't see me going out with him anytime soon. At least not in this lifetime."

"For someone who's so *forward thinking*, you can sure be pretty shallow sometimes," says Felicia.

I feel a sense of relief that Amy's irritating question about cheerleaders got lost in the shuffle as the two of them banter back and forth for a while.

"Yeah, yeah," says Amy. My relief vanishes as she sticks her pen back in my face now. "But let's get back to my question for Kara here. And I don't expect you be so evasive this time. The press wants to know your opinion on this year's cheerleaders. And is it true that you used to actually be friends with one of them?"

Just then Edgar reappears, flopping the big pizza box down on the table and giving us all napkins. "Jump in!"

As we're eating pizza, Amy turns back to me. "Don't think you're getting off the hook that easy," she persists, grabbing up her pen and pointing it to me again. "The press wants to know what you think of this year's cheerleaders."

I roll my eyes at her then speak into her mike. "I think I know what the press is getting at, and, as a matter of fact, I used to know one of the cheerleaders personally. But she and I have parted ways."

Amy nods and reaches for another slice of veggie pizza. "Uh-huh. And would the fact that she's suddenly a *popular* cheerleader and running with the, uh"—she makes a gagging sound—"*cool* kids have anything to do with this, uh, unexpected split?"

I sigh and consider an answer as I take a bite of pizza. Which route to take here? Honesty, and risk more public humiliation? Or sarcasm, and hope for an escape from this line of questioning. I finally decide to take the safer road. I sit up straighter and try to appear somewhat intellectual. "Actually, Ms. Weatherspoon, I feel that I have outgrown the ridiculous Jordan Ferguson and her never-ending need for fans and approval. I say if girls have to jump up and down, giggling and jiggling like a bunch of bimbos, and if they have to bare their flesh and flash their smiles just to win their popularity, well, I'd rather not have anything to do with them in the first place."

"Here! Here!" yells Amy as she lifts up her water bottle in the form of a toast. "Way to go, girl."

Felicia is frowning slightly. "Sounds like you really hate your old friend."

I shrug. "It's a two-way street."

"Ah-hah!" says Amy as if she's finally struck the mother lode. "So she did dump you after all?"

"Aw, come on, you guys," says Edgar. "Let's drop it. It's obvious that Kara wants to move on."

I glance at this strange kid and feel an unexpected wave of grat-itude. For a nerd, he seems pretty thoughtful. "This is good pizza, Edgar," I tell him, eager to change the subject. "Thanks."

He grins. "We really didn't invite you to join us just so that Amy could torture you. She's just like that, you know. She gets her kicks from making other people feel uncomfortable."

Amy points at him now. "You should be thankful for the dis-traction, Eddie. I could be going after you today."

"Not when I treat for pizza," he says with surprising authority. "Don't we have some kind of unspoken agreement that you lay off on pizza days?"

She nods. "Yeah, you're right about that. Besides, we needed to initiate Kara."

"Don't let Amy scare you, Kara," says Felicia. "We're not always like this. Some days we just sit in here in absolute silence and eat and do art."

"Yeah, and some days I make an effort to wake these guys up," says Amy. "Someone has to."

Well, I feel more awake today than I've felt all week. But I'm not sure which I like better—sleepwalking or being jolted back to my unfortunate reality by someone like Amy Weatherspoon. The truth is, Amy scares me a little. She's like this loose cannon and you never know who she'll blast next. Felicia, on the other hand, feels much more even-keeled. I'm guessing she keeps the lunch bunch balanced and from killing each other. I'm not quite sure what to think about Edgar anymore. At first, I'd written him off as a nerd and a goofball. Now, I think I may have been too hasty and misjudged him. I'm curious as to who he really is and what he really thinks.

As I walk home from school, by myself as usual, I try to imagine what Jordan would say about my new friends. Okay, calling them *friends* is probably stretching it. But at least they included me today. Or sort of. But I can just imagine Jordan's take on Amy. She'd probably chime in with her new friends: "Goth Girl," "fashion disaster," "garage-sale geek," "witchy wannabe," and all sorts of other mean and unflattering things. More interestingly, I wonder what Amy would say to them—especially if she knew the kinds of things they say about her. Maybe she does know. Maybe that's why she is the way she is.

And then there's Edgar. Oh man, I can just imagine how Jordan would react to him. "See, Kara," she would say to me (if we were talking, that is), "I told you those art kids were nerds and geeks and freaks. And that Edgar Peebles, give me a break! He's the nerdiest geek of them all. I'll bet he even picks his nose."

Of course, I take some satisfaction in linking myself up with the kind of kids that Jordan would *not* approve of. I almost wish the art lunch bunch would consider me their friend now, just so I could flaunt them in front of Jordan—perhaps even embarrass her in front of her shallow new friends. Amber would probably say something like, "I can't believe you used to hang with that loser girl, Jordan. Just look at her and her weird little friends. What a bunch of geeks!"

Even the neatly dressed and academic Felicia Wong would draw their poison darts—perhaps even more than the others, I think as I approach my apartment. They would pick on her the most simply because she is closer to being like them than Edgar or Amy. It hits me as I go up the stairs that this is really true. The "cool" kids can laugh and joke casually about kids who are "out there" so far that they're not anything close to a threat. But when other kids wear clothes that are similar, or heaven forbid, *the same* as the popular kids—watch out! It's weird really. And I wonder if the bigger world is going to be anything like this. And, if so, what's the use? If people are going to be so hard on each other, so mean, so superficial, why put up with all the pain? Why not just go off to some deserted island or a cabin in the woods and become a hermit?

I'll tell you why. It's simple. I couldn't stand the loneliness. I can't. It's eating me alive.

eleven

OKAY, JORDAN WOULD SAY THAT I'M DESPERATE AND PATHETIC, AND maybe I am, but I have stayed with the art bunch during lunchtime every day of this entire week. First of all, I think it was amazing that I survived the previous weekend. I was so lonely and blue on Friday night that I wanted to go jump off a bridge somewhere. Unfortunately (or fortunately, depending on how you look at it), we don't have any good bridges in our town.

So that's when I decided to read a book that my grandmother had sent me last summer. "For your summer reading," she'd written on a sweet little card with daisies on it. Like I actually read books in the summertime. At least not last summer, when I had a friend to hang with and places to go. (Well, when I wasn't babysitting for the neighbor's two grade-school-aged kids.)

Anyway, I'm not even sure what made me pick up this paper-back in the first place. Boredom I suppose. I could tell right off that it was a "religious" sort of book. And I know that my grandma is really into her church these days. More so than ever since my grandpa died last winter. But this particular book was about a teenage girl who became a Christian when she was sixteen then died in a car wreck exactly one year later (she was wiped out by a drunken driver). Okay, to start with, I was thinking, *Now this is a cheerful little book. Not!* But I must admit that something about it was intriguing. And I found myself getting caught up in the story and this girl's life and I actually cried when it ended.

Plus it gave me a lot to chew on and think about. And I've been wanting to share some of these thoughts with my new art "friends." Okay, I'm still not sure that I can call them friends. For one thing, we don't spend time together outside of art. Also, they all seem to have their own circles of friends. Amy has her pot-smoking Goth group. And Felicia has a couple of academic chums that she's hung with since middle school. Even Edgar has a life. He's in chess club and goes to some kind of youth group. So calling myself their friend is still really stretching it. Just the same, I've stayed in the art room during lunch every day this week. I've been the brunt of Amy's attacks, been defended by Edgar, and listened to Felicia's soapbox lectures. I've watched as a couple of other kids have dropped in and out during the course of the week. But I can tell that the core art lunch bunch consists of Amy, Felicia, and Edgar. And on Friday it's just the three of them and me again.

I had already offered to spring for pizza today, and Edgar called it in and went out to meet the pizza van on the street. I had saved up a week's worth of lunch money by packing my own lunches, and I thought it'd be good to spend it on this. No one argued with my offer either. Not even Edgar, although I'm sure he knows this means Amy has open season on him.

I'm into my second slice when I decide to bring up the subject that's bugging me. I sense that Felicia will have something definite to say about it. Maybe Edgar too. For that matter, I'm sure Amy will have an opinion.

"I read this book," I begin. "About a girl who's about our age, but she gets killed by a drunken driver."

"Nice," says Amy with sarcasm. "Guess we don't need to read it now that we know how the story ends. Thanks."

"Actually the book cover makes that perfectly clear," I continue. "The thing is, this girl supposedly has a personal relationship with God during this year. She writes about it in her journal, and her parents find it afterward, and that's mainly what the book's about."

"I think I read that," says Felicia eagerly. "Is it called *Last Dance*?"

"Yeah."

"I totally loved that book!"

"Really? It left me feeling kind of confused."

"Confused?" says Amy. "Sounds more like it would leave you feeling depressed."

"Depends on how you look at it," says Felicia.

I frown. "Maybe it's just me. But I found it pretty hard to believe. Do you think it's really true?"

"True?" echoes Felicia. "True as in did this really happen? Did that girl become a Christian, keep a journal, and then get killed?"

I shrug. That's not exactly what I meant.

"Yeah, I think that's true," says Felicia. "Why would they make it up?"

"Not that so much. I mean do you think it's true that you can really have a close relationship with God? That you can talk to him and have him talk back to you and everything? That just seems pretty far-fetched to me."

The room gets quiet now and it seems that Felicia is stumped.

"I think you can," says Edgar finally.

"Oh, no, here we go," says Amy. "Thanks a lot, Kara!"

Edgar adjusts his glasses then glances over at Felicia. "I know that you and I believe pretty much the same things, but I guess I take it more seriously."

"Maybe," says Felicia. "But it's no secret that I'm a Christian. I just don't go over the top like some people."

"Over the top?" I venture.

She shrugs. "Let Edgar explain."

He smiles. "Yeah, Felicia sometimes thinks that I'm a religious fanatic. And maybe I am. I just happen to believe in God and Jesus Christ and the Bible. And I think that you can have a personal relationship with God when you invite Jesus into your heart. It's not that complicated, really. It's just what I personally believe. I have no reason not to."

"See the can of worms you just opened, Kara," says Amy as she reaches for another piece of pizza.

I'm not quite sure what she means.

"I believe in most of that too," offers Felicia. "But Edgar's right. I don't take it as seriously he does. He goes to church about five times a week."

He holds up three fingers. "Not quite."

"Still." Felicia shakes her head. "Three times a week. I'm doing good to make it on Sundays. Not only that, but Edgar reads his Bible every single day. Maybe he reads it twice a day. And he prays all the time."

I'm looking at Edgar now like he's someone from another planet. Can that really be true? Can a normal person possibly read the Bible and pray and go to church *that much?* Of course, I remember, Edgar's not exactly normal.

"And I'm not saying it's a bad thing," continues Felicia. "In some ways I admire him. I'm just not like that."

"And that's okay," says Edgar. "It's good to be different. God made us all unique people. For me it's the right thing to do. I need to go to church a lot and read a lot and pray a lot. It's like breathing air and eating food. My spirit requires these things. But Felicia seems to be doing just fine with the way she's living too."

She makes a funny grin. "Thanks."

"No, really, I mean it. I admire you too."

"Oh, man!" says Amy with a dramatic rolling of the eyes. "You guys are gonna make me lose my lunch."

"Sorry," I say quickly, feeling like I'm in way over my head here anyway. "I didn't mean to get us all involved in a religious discussion. I just wondered what you thought about that."

"I think it's a bunch of hooey," says Amy, taking another slice of veggie pizza and stringing the cheese around her finger. "I say, live and let live. And if there really is a God up there, then why'd he let the world turn into such a pathetic mess? I say, he must've fallen asleep at the wheel. Or he's like the guy in that book you just read, driving drunk and about to kill another innocent bystander along the way."

"Oh, Amy," says Felicia.

"Don't worry," says Edgar. "God's a big boy. He can take it."

"What makes you so sure?" I ask.

"I just know inside here." He taps on his chest and smiles. "Some things have to be experienced before you really understand. Faith is like that."

"Well, I don't get it." I reach for another piece of pizza.

"Faith is like walking through a door you've never seen before. You don't know what's on the other side until you walk through. People can tell you, but you won't get it. You just have to go and see for yourself."

Felicia nods now. "I have to agree with him there. Getting to know God is a personal journey that's different for everyone."

I'm sure I look more confused than ever, and Amy pats me

reassuringly on the back. "Hey, don't worry, Kara. I seriously doubt that God, if he's really there, even gives a rip what we think one way or another. Religion is just this game that people made up a long time ago when they had too much time on their hands and no good movies to see."

Then the buzzer rings and we begin to clean up our pizza mess, leaving the two leftover pieces for Ms. Clark.

"She likes it when we do that," explains Felicia as we arrange the pizza with a little note. "She usually spends her lunch break running over to visit her mom in the nursing home and doesn't have time to eat anyway."

For the first time Felicia and I walk together from the art room. "So, what are you doing this weekend?" she asks.

"I don't know."

"I heard about an art show at the university that I'd like to go see on Saturday. It's American Impressionists and it's supposed to be good. You want to come?"

"Sure, I guess so."

So I give her my phone number and address and she promises to pick me up around eleven on Saturday. I am curious as to how she plans to pick me up because she, like me, is only a sophomore, but I suppose it's possible she's already turned sixteen and has her license. Anyway, I'm so thankful that I have something to do this weekend that I don't even care if her great-grandmother is driving us.

Feeling slightly better about life, I continue on toward my next class. Naturally, I notice that Jordan and her pack of friends are clustered together like a flock of sheep in the middle of the hallway. They are unavoidable. Forcing everyone else to walk around them as they take up more than their fair share of space, they act like they think they own the place. And maybe they do, for all I know. Maybe when you become a cheerleader you are given a secret set of keys to the entire high school, perhaps even the town, maybe the universe too.

It is so aggravating to see Jordan now, just when I was beginning to feel almost normal. It's like seeing her just jangles my nerves or rattles my brain. It's like that feeling you get when someone honks a horn unexpectedly or pops a balloon right in your ear. It's just completely unsettling.

So I take a deep breath, trying to calm myself as I go out of my way to walk *around* this clog of stupid cheerleaders. Now it's not that I expect Jordan to stop chattering with her friends and say "hi" to me or even carry on the most superficial of conversations. I fully realize that we are far beyond that now. But at the same time it just feels so weird to be so utterly ignored by a girl who was once closer than a sister. And it still hurts me deep inside to remember that I once trusted this person with all my secrets, hopes, and dreams. It makes me feel stupid and vulnerable and weak. And I hate it!

I see her eyes dart toward me, then back to Shawna, who, judging by the high-pitched squeals of laughter, appears to be telling the funniest story of all times. I can tell that Jordan saw me though. And I know by that look in her eye that she wished she hadn't. I suspect that nothing would make Jordan happier than if I were to just — now you see her, now you don't, *poof* — disappear from the face of the planet without the slightest trace. Then no one could ever say to her, "Oh, Jordan, there goes that poor loser of a girl that you used to be friends with. What on earth were you thinking?"

For I am certain that I am a bone of contention for Jordan Ferguson. I am that hideous and embarrassing remnant of her less than illustrious and not very popular past, a living reminder that Jordan Ferguson isn't quite as cool as she'd like to be.

twelve

I GET UP EARLY ON SATURDAY TO GO RUNNING. IT'S NOT HARD TO DO since I stayed home, again, on a Friday night last night. There was a football game, but I couldn't bring myself to go. Like that old Carly Simon song goes, "I haven't got time for the pain." But this morning, I am thinking more positively about my life.

As I run through our still-sleeping town, I am hoping that perhaps Felicia and I are going to become good friends, starting today. Maybe even best friends eventually. It could happen. I realize she's very different from Jordan, and I'm okay with that. In some ways I think she is more trustworthy, since she seems a little more grounded and down-to-earth. I realize that she might not be as fun or crazy as Jordan. But at the same time I don't think she's the kind of girl who would dump a friend just because she suddenly became "popular." Still, you never know. From here on out, I will proceed with caution.

I change my clothes several times before it's time for Felicia to pick me up. I tell myself this is really stupid. We're only going to an art show for pity's sake. And Felicia doesn't seem to be into fashion, at least not like Jordan is. But it seems so important to me to look perfect. I am so lame. You'd think I was going out on a date or something. Finally I settle on something safe. Khakis and a black turtleneck sweater. I tell myself that it looks a little bit artsy.

And really, I look pretty good in this sweater.

Around eleven I decide to go downstairs and wait. I'm not really ready for Felicia to see where I live yet. Not that I'm ashamed of our apartment. Mom has worked hard to make it look fairly decent, even though her taste in décor isn't my first choice. But still it's small compared to most kids' houses (or so I assume). I know it's about a quarter of the size of the Ferguson home.

Finally a yellow Mustang pulls up and I see Felicia waving from the passenger side. I run over and wait for her to get out so that I can climb into the back.

"Do you know Jessie?" asks Felicia as she hops back inside.

"Yeah," I say from the backseat. "Jessie Rubenstein, you're a junior, right?"

The brown-haired girl behind the wheel nods. "Yeah, I think I remember you from middle school. Weren't you good friends with Jordan Ferguson?"

"Yeah, I used to be."

"She's doing a good job as a cheerleader. Did you go to the game last night?"

"No, I had something else to do," I say, thinking, *Yeah sure, like I had to stay home and wash my hair.*

"The cheerleaders did a pretty cool routine at halftime," said Jessie. "Jordan was impressive."

"Uh-huh."

"Jessie's not really into art," says Felicia quickly. I wonder if she realizes how this conversation about my ex-best friend is making me uncomfortable. "But I talked her into coming. Don't you just love her car? If it gets warmer out maybe we can talk her into putting the top down. Can you believe that her parents got this for her sixteenth birthday?"

"Well, I have to work to pay for the insurance," injects Jessie as she enters the freeway. "And that's not cheap."

"Man, I wish I could have it so hard," teases Felicia. "My parents are so overly protective that I probably won't even be able to get my license when I turn sixteen. And they would never in a million years get me a car as cool as this."

I want to ask how they know each other. Are they neighbors or what? For some reason it seems odd to think of being close friends with someone a year older. But then what do I know about these things?

Then Jessie puts in a J. Lo CD and cranks it up so that conversation becomes impossible. I am relieved, since I really can't think of anything very impressive to say. I'm a little taken aback by Jessie's presence. I had imagined that it would be just Felicia and me hanging together and getting better acquainted.

The art exhibit is pretty good. But I find myself feeling more and more like an outsider as I follow behind Felicia and Jessie. In Felicia's defense, she's trying to get Jessie interested in art by explaining some things to her. Still, it makes me feel like a fifth wheel or maybe, since there are three of us, it should be third wheel, although that sounds more like a tricycle to me and rather childish.

Just the same, I try not to think about this too much as I look at the paintings and try to study the techniques. Besides my dad's paintings at home, I've never really been this close to real art before, and it's kind of exciting. Some of the paintings are really amazing, and I wonder what it must've felt like to create something so incredible. I feel that I am getting more and more pulled into art. It's like something deep inside of me responds to it in a way that totally surprises me. Like there's this mysterious magnet that's tugging on my heart.

As I walk slowly down the aisles of paintings, I wonder if I would have what it takes to become a serious artist. Although I take it somewhat for granted, I realize that my father was pretty artistic. Besides the painting over the couch, we still have a metal sculpture and a couple of smaller paintings in our house. But now I want to go home and study them more closely. It's like I'm getting a fresh set of eyes when it comes to art.

I guess one reason I never think too much about my dad being an artist is because I've heard over and over about how his art was one of the main reasons their marriage broke up, which is slightly ironic since I've heard my mom tell other people that it was his art that attracted her to him in the first place. And she still likes his art and keeps it in our apartment. I guess it was the financial part of life that finally did them in. Apparently my dad had a hard time holding down a regular job with a regular paycheck. He preferred doing art, and according to Mom, although he had talent, his art did *not* pay the bills. Finally, she got tired of supporting him and bickering about money all the time, and eventually she kicked him out and when he didn't come back she just filed for a divorce. And that was that.

Other than my parents fighting and yelling a lot, I barely remember those days. I was only five when they split, and I suppose I might have some sort of psychological block going on inside of me. When I was little, I used to always imagine that my father would come back to us and we'd all live happily ever after. But the years kept going by and he never did. To be perfectly honest, other than those times when I look at the painting over our couch, I rarely even think of him anymore. Or when I do, it's not exactly happy thoughts. I suppose I've been angry at him for a lot of things over the years. I've held him personally responsible for stuff that's gone wrong in my life, and our lack of finances, and even when my mom's all grouchy. It's hard to say whether or not these things are his fault, but it's easy to blame someone who's not around to defend himself.

It occurs to me now that I have absolutely no idea whether or not he still pursues art. In fact, I know virtually nothing about the man. But with all my recent exposure to art, I'm beginning to feel surprisingly curious. I even begin to examine the names of the artists more carefully, almost expecting to spy the name Michael Hendricks among them. Of course, I know this is somewhat ridiculous since, as far as I know, my father was only into "modern" art.

Finally, I think we've seen everything there is to see and I'm feeling overwhelmed.

"Do you want to get some lunch?" asks Jessie as we stand on the steps outside of the art exhibit.

"Sure," I answer. Then I hope that I have enough money not to embarrass myself in case they decide to go someplace nice. I get the impression that Jessie is pretty well-off, and I think I only have about five bucks on me after paying for admission to the art exhibit. I had stupidly assumed it would be free.

Fortunately we settle for fast food and my five bucks is plenty. But as we sit there eating, I feel even more like an outsider. It's not as if Felicia and Jessie are intentionally excluding me. But as they laugh and chat comfortably together, I begin to suspect they've been friends for years.

"How long have you guys been friends?" I ask when the conversation finally comes to a lull.

"Oh, man, we've known each other since diaper days," says Jessie as she dips a fry in ketchup. "Actually, I might've been out of diapers, but Felicia was probably still a Pampers girl."

Felicia laughs. "Yeah, our parents are really good friends. My dad works for Jessie's dad and they play golf every Saturday. Our moms went to college together and, despite our obvious ethnical differences, it feels like we're all related." She grins at Jessie now. "Which is kind of nice since I'm an only child and most of our other relatives live pretty far away. Quite a few are still in China. But the Rubensteins have always been like family to us."

"That's cool," I say. And it is. I'm happy for them. Really, I am. There's nothing like having a best friend that you've known for years. *Nothing.*

Jessie decides to put the top down on the way home, and I imagine I am having a really great time. Three girls riding down the freeway in a convertible. Hair blowing in the wind, guys in cars waving at us. But the truth is I feel miserable. Sitting by myself in the backseat, I feel left out and lonelier than ever.

Still, when we reach my apartment complex, I force a big smile and thank them both for including me today. I tell Felicia how much I loved the art exhibit, and Jessie how much I love her car. Then I wave goodbye and jog toward the stairs of my apartment. I hope that my effort at cheerfulness is convincing because when I get safely to the privacy of my room I begin to cry again.

I wonder if this sadness will ever end. Just when I think I'm doing better, it's like the rug gets pulled out from under me. I see the book that I read last week sitting on my dresser. I think about the girl, Alicia, who gave her heart to God and supposedly had a personal relationship with him. I wonder if that's really even possible. It's not that I don't believe in God. Usually, I do. I'm just never sure what I think beyond that. Still, I was impressed with the way Alicia's year went. Well, other than dying in the end. That was kind of a downer. But during that year preceding her death, she made lots of great friends and had a really good life. In her journal she kept saying it was the best year of her entire life. She was so totally happy and in love with life and God and everyone. And it had been a real change for her, because it sounded like she'd been pretty miserable before. Sort of like me.

So I've been sitting here just wondering. What if I were to give my heart to God? What if I did like Alicia and it caused my life to really get better? I even wonder if that's what it would take to get Jordan back as my best friend. I know that Jordan's family goes to church. But not every Sunday since her dad's pretty laid back about the whole thing and has no problem telling anyone that he would just as soon spend a Sunday at the lake as in church. I also know that Jordan believes in God and calls herself a Christian. But she's never really been too involved in church. And she doesn't go to the youth group because she says that the kids there are nerds.

Suddenly it's pretty tempting to give this God-thing a shot. I mean, what do I have to lose? And what if it made my life go back to the way it used to be, only better? Wouldn't that be worth a lot? I am beginning to feel hopeful. Perhaps I have found the answer after all.

Yet, at the same time, I feel like I might be just playing a game with fate here. Sort of like a holy "Let's Make a Deal." And that kind of scares me. I'm thinking that if God is really for real, and if he can really make you or break you, well, I could be playing with fire here. And I've got to wonder whether it's worth the risk of blowing it with God just because I think I might be able to swing some sort of deal. I mean if *I* were God and some goofy girl was down there trying to strike up a bargain with me, well, how would that make *me* feel? So, I suppose I should give this some more thought before I jump into anything.

Because the sorry truth is my life is cruddy enough without going and making it worse by messing with someone like God.

thirteen

I SPENT ALL DAY SUNDAY BABYSITTING FOR THE NEIGHBORS, WHICH WAS better than moping around and feeling sorry for myself. Plus I earned a little spending money. Not that I have anything to spend it on. I've discovered that one must have a life to need money. I suppose that could be one of the upsides of being friendless. I could become rich in time.

Now it is Monday and I am trudging back to school, wishing that I were someplace else, or someone else, or had someone else for a best friend.

As I walk into the school I notice a boy that I've always thought was cute. His name is Jeremy Thatcher and I've known him since grade school. He's standing by the bulletin board at the entrance, probably trying to look inconspicuous, like he's actually reading the dribble posted up there. He's one of the shiest kids I've ever known. Even if you only say "hi" to him his face turns beet red. But he's also very nice.

"Hey, Jeremy," I say, waiting to see him blush.

"Hey," he says in a quiet voice. Then he glances away as if something more important than the bulletin board has captured his attention. But I'm not disappointed because a couple of bright pink spots suddenly appear on his cheeks.

Feeling slightly mean, I push things a bit further. "How you doing?" I ask, walking right up to him.

"Uh, okay."

"Did you get your economics report done?" I ask. He's in that class with me.

"Yeah."

"Pretty boring, huh?"

He nods without speaking now.

I'm thinking I've pushed Jeremy about as far as is safe. So I give him my best smile and tell him to have a good day.

To my surprise, he smiles back and says, "Thanks, Kara."

Wow, I'm thinking as I head toward English, *maybe, if I worked really, really hard at this, maybe I could actually strike up some sort of relationship with this guy.* I'm thinking maybe I should quit hoping for a girl to be my best friend and just go after a guy instead. I've never really had a serious boyfriend before. Oh, I've gone with a few guys. Okay, maybe only two. And these were both a result of Jordan setting me up with people who were friends with the guys that she liked. A convenience thing. But these relationships felt awkward and were short-lived and even sort of silly when you think about it.

But what if Jeremy and I became a thing? Already I am imagining us together. Walking to class together. Hanging together in the hallway. Maybe even kissing? I imagine Jeremy saving me a spot at lunch and taking me to the games and dances. And suddenly this sounds like a perfect solution to my miserable little life.

The problem is that I'm just not sure how to go about it. Because even though everyone knows that Jeremy is extremely shy, I happen to know that I am probably only a few degrees less shy than him. And what I did this morning was pretty out of character for me. At least I *think* it is. Lately, I'm not too sure about much. But what if I could change myself? Or maybe I already am changing and I just don't know it. Maybe I don't have the foggiest idea of who I am.

I find a seat by the only window and ponder these thoughts all through English class, which now means I have *homework*. But I don't care about this as I hurry toward my next class, economics. I am hoping to catch another word with Jeremy now, maybe even sit by him and make my best attempt to flirt. So I linger by the door, pretending to study a paper in my hand until I finally see Jeremy approach. As usual, he keeps his eyes downward and doesn't even see me. But that's okay. I'm up to the challenge.

"Hi, Jeremy," I say again, trying my best smile.

His cheeks begin to flame again and this time he mutters a barely audible greeting, then ducking his head back down, he goes into the classroom and heads for the back row. And before I can nab the desk beside him it is taken by Jonathon Knight, an overweight boy who's nearly as shy as Jeremy. I wonder if they have some sort of secret pact or club. Shy Boys United.

I take the desk a couple seats away from Jeremy and spend the best part of the next hour trying to get his attention. However, I fail miserably and as soon as class is over, Jeremy makes a beeline for the door. I'm sure I have scared this poor boy to death. I find this ironic since I consider myself the shy person in most social settings. I wonder what Jordan would think if she knew what I was up to. Most likely she couldn't care less.

I watch for Jeremy between classes but finally decide he is trying to avoid me. I'm not sure if this has anything to do with me personally, or if it is just because of his extreme shyness. Or maybe he's gay.

"Hi, Kara," says a guy's voice.

I turn, hoping that perhaps it's the mysterious Jeremy, then frown to see that it's only Edgar.

"Hey, Edgar," I say as I walk with him toward the art room. "What's up?"

"Not much. Did you go to that art exhibit with Felicia?"

"Yeah, it was really good. Did you get to see it?"

"Nah, our church was having a missions conference this weekend and I had to stick around to help."

"What's a missions conference?" I ask as we go sit at the back table in the art room. I've taken up sitting in the back now so I don't have to move my stuff at lunchtime.

"Our church supports a few missionaries in other countries. And once a year we invite them or someone else to come in and talk about foreign missions."

I frown at him. "You mean like people who go to places like Africa and try to force the people there to wear clothes and go to church?"

He laughs. "Not exactly. The kinds of missions that our church supports do things like teaching people to read and building houses and digging wells."

"Oh."

"I think God is calling me to be a missionary," he tells me now.

I just stare at him in wonder. He could be telling me that God had invited him to step onto a UFO and go live on Mars and I wouldn't be any more surprised. "You actually *heard* God *calling* to you?" I ask skeptically as I pull out my current art project.

But then Ms. Clark begins to talk and our conversation comes to a fast stop. A relief, I'm thinking, since I really don't want to get involved in a discussion like this.

However, as soon as lunchtime rolls around, Edgar brings up the subject again.

"I wanted to answer your question, Kara," he begins as we all start taking out our lunches. Mine is a raisin bagel and carton of lemon yogurt.

"What was her question?" asks Amy.

"She wanted to know if I could actually hear God calling me to be a missionary."

Amy groaned loudly. "Oh, man, do we *have* to talk about religion today? My Jesus-freak aunt stayed at our house all weekend and I have been preached to up to here." She held her hand high in the air to demonstrate.

"Hey, I'm with you," I agree. "I was just making conversation with Edgar. I'm not looking for a sermon either."

She sighs in relief. "Okay, let's talk about the art exhibit on campus. Did you guys go?"

So Edgar is quieted, and the three of us girls monopolize the conversation by talking about the exhibit.

"But here's the best part," says Amy in an excited voice, for Amy anyway. "I met this really cool guy at the exhibit. His name is Leon and he's in college, majoring in art. And he actually thought I was in college too. Of course, I didn't tell him I wasn't. Anyway, we really hit it off. And I had the coolest weekend. It was awesome."

"Are you going to see him again?" asks Felicia, her brow furrowed with concern.

"Of course." Amy looks at Felicia like she's crazy.

"But what about your age differ—"

"That doesn't matter. The important thing is we're soul mates. Age has nothing to do with it, Felicia!"

I can see that Amy's getting irritated here, and I decide to jump in and see if I can keep things calm. "I wish I was in college," I say. Now, this isn't untrue.

"Me too," agrees Amy. "People are so juvenile in high school."

"Not me," says Felicia. "I think high school is great. Actually, I think it's what you make it. And if you can't make it good in high school, I doubt that you can make it much better in college."

Amy glares at Felicia now. "Well, high school might work for some kids. Like kids who have a high-school mentality. But it's *not* for everyone."

"It's a lot better than middle school," offers Edgar. "I really hated middle school. Kids were a whole lot meaner there."

"Yeah," I agree with him, hoping to make up for cutting him off about his hearing-God thing. "I think there's something inherently vicious about that age group. Man, you couldn't get me to go back to that era for anything."

"Anyone going to the Harvest Dance?" asks Felicia.

"Are you?" I ask her in surprise. I'm not aware that she has a boyfriend.

She nods. "You bet."

"Who are you going with?" I ask.

Amy laughs. "Don't you know about Felicia's old standby?"

"Huh?"

"We're not really dating regularly," explains Felicia with what looks like a tiny bit of embarrassment. "But we have this agreement to go to dances and things together unless the other one is dating someone else."

"It's like having your brother take you to the dance," says Amy with one raised brow. "Kinda weird if you ask me."

"No one's asking," says Felicia. Then she turns to me. "I'm going with Aaron Rubenstein. He's a senior."

"Jessie's brother?"

Felicia nods. "He's a nice guy who drives a nice car, and Jessie and her boyfriend are doubling with us."

"Convenient," says Amy as if it's a disgusting arrangement.

"Hey, it works for us. And it's better than pretending to be in college to hook up with some desperate old guy."

Fortunately this makes Amy laugh. I sigh with relief.

Amy slaps Felicia on the back now. "Hey, I'm sorry to be on your case. I guess my Bible-thumping aunt just put me in a bad mood. It's a free country and you can go out with whoever you please."

Then the bell rings and we clean up our lunch stuff and all go our separate ways. As I walk toward the math department I feel a surprising wave of jealousy as I consider Felicia's "convenient little arrangement." I wish that my family had connections like that. In some ways, I used to have that with Jordan.

Even though Jordan and I both agreed that the Harvest Dance was "totally stupid" last year, I'll bet all my babysitting money that she plans to go this year. And if I was still her best friend I'd probably be going too. Oh, life is so unfair!

On my way home from school, I briefly toy with the idea of walking up to Jeremy Thatcher and just inviting him to go to the Harvest Dance with me. I try to convince myself this would be quite the liberated thing for me to do. But, of course, I realize that it only shows how pathetically desperate I am. Still I can't help but run the possibility through my mind. But the more I think about it, the more I realize it's totally lame.

For starters, poor Jeremy would probably drop over dead if I actually asked him out. But then, if by some miracle he accepted, he'd probably be so paralyzed with fear that he'd be completely and embarrassingly dysfunctional at the dance. I can imagine myself stuck on the sidelines with the red-faced immovable boy. And more than likely, we'd be the brunt of everyone's jokes too. "Look at those two social rejects over there." "Who do they think they're fooling?" I can especially imagine the kinds of things that Jordan's little crowd might say. Subtle little jabs that they would quietly snicker at among themselves.

Besides that, how would we get to the stupid dance in the first place? I've only seen Jeremy riding a bike to school and around town. I seriously doubt that he's even old enough to drive yet. Maybe, I thought, his parents could drive us. Sheesh, I don't even know why I bother my brain with such ridiculous ideas.

fourteen

I EXCHANGE MY DREAMS OF JEREMY FOR THE REMOTE CONTROL AS I FLOP down on the sofa with a can of cream soda. Dr. Bill's pop psychology talk show is on after school every day and lately I've become something of an addict. I suppose that watching other people with their own problems, often much more serious than mine, is somewhat reassuring. Or else I'm just such a loser that I have nothing better to do.

Today Dr. Bill is hitting pretty close to home and it's starting to make me a little uncomfortable. He's talking about daughters with absent fathers. And I suppose that would describe me. Still, it's not something I like to think about too much. I mean, what good does it really do?

"When was the last time you saw your father?" Dr. Bill asks a woman who looks to be in her twenties.

"I was about seven," she answers.

"And you're okay with that?" Dr. Bill looks as if he's skeptical.

"Yeah. I missed him at first, but then I moved on with my life."

"So why are you here then?"

She looks over to the audience. "My mom thinks I have a problem."

"A problem?" echoes Dr. Bill. I've noticed he does this a lot. I can't tell if he's trying to buy time or just hoping to make his guests a little uncomfortable.

"Yeah, with relationships."

"With guys?"

"Yeah, I guess so."

"Well, according to your mother, you have some real serious problems with your relationships with guys. Let's roll the video."

Fade to video. An older woman, I'm guessing the mother, is explaining how her daughter moves from guy to guy to guy, how she's never able to make a commitment and always looking for the perfect guy.

"I'm afraid she's ruining her life," says the mom as she literally wrings her hands. "She's a lovely girl, but this relentless search for her father is making her miserable."

Now the camera is back on the girl again. And she is quietly crying.

"Do you think that's true?" asks Dr. Bill.

"I don't know."

"Do you think you're looking for someone to take the place of your missing father?"

She nods now, with tears streaming down her cheeks. I feel a lump growing in my throat and realize I can't take it anymore. I lift the remote and turn off the TV.

I stand up and turn on the spotlight above the painting that hangs over the stone sofa. I've been studying it a lot lately. At first I thought I was trying to understand it from an artistic perspective. But now I realize it's something more. I think that if I stare at it long enough or hard enough, I might actually figure out who my dad really is and why he couldn't get it together with his family. But it's not working.

The painting consists of about five colors. Mostly black and white swirls and splatters, with a few splashes of blue and red and yellow on top. I guess it's an abstract, which is probably why it doesn't make any sense to me. Then there's this shiny red ball in the lower left-hand corner. But what does it mean? Does it mean that the world is a squiggly, mixed-up mess of color and darkness and light? Is the red ball in the corner symbolic of something? My dad? His pain? His heart? What???

After looking at this frustrating painting for a while, my head begins to throb. I'm not sure if it's because I'm thinking so hard or because my eyes are just getting strained from trying to untangle the mess. Finally I just look away and my eyes thank me. I haven't done any better with his other paintings or even his sculpture. The bronze piece that sits on the table in the hallway appears to be something between a horse, a dog, and a man, although it's all con-glomerated together in one big mesh of metal. Everything my dad created appears to be tangled and twisted and mixed up and messy. What does it mean?

If my dad was around I could ask him. And I could ask him to explain what he was thinking when he made these frustrating images. And what was he thinking when he walked out of our lives and never came back. And what I am supposed to do with my messed up life now. I wonder if my dad was painting about me and my life. Maybe he was a prophet. Maybe he knew that I was going to turn out to be a mess. Or maybe I'm just like him.

I consider asking my mom some questions about my dad, but then I remember the last time I asked. I was about twelve and curi-ous about my roots. But my questions eventually drove my mom to tears and I never really did get to the bottom of it. Finally, I just gave up and promised myself to never do that again. Still, I wonder. I even consider writing him a letter. I could pour out my heart to him and send it—where? I wouldn't have a clue. I wonder if I should go online and see if I can find him. But what if he doesn't want to be found? What if he rejects me—*again?* I don't think I could handle it. It might ruin me for life.

I grab up the remote, hurrying to turn Dr. Bill back on, since I realize now that I desperately need to know what he was saying to those poor fatherless women. But it's too late, the dorky end-of-the-show music is already playing and he's winding down. I chastise myself for turning it off too soon. I might've actually learned something useful.

I watch as Dr. Bill talks about tomorrow's show, but I mute the sound now and I study this small, slightly bald middle-aged guy with kind blue eyes behind wire-rimmed glasses and I wonder what it would be like to have a dad like that. I imagine Dr. Bill coming home from work and asking me about my day. I would tell him everything about Jordan dumping me and how my life sucks, and I'm sure he would hug me and come up with all the perfect answers. I'm sure he could put me all back together again. I actually toy with the idea of writing Dr. Bill a letter and asking him if he will adopt me, although I realize it's ridiculous. I'm too old for that sort of thing and I'm sure it would hurt my mom's feelings. Besides, he probably gets thousands of letters like that every single day. I would be just one more hopeless loser, lost in the great big pile of *pitiful*.

My week continues, one boring day following the next. Nothing seems to change and nothing gets any better. I've become an expert at avoiding Jordan and her ridiculous friends. Sometimes I wonder if she ever thinks about me anymore. Does she think that I have simply vanished? Or perhaps transferred to another school? Or died of a broken heart? Does she even care?

I saw Jordan's dad picking her up at school one afternoon. He was standing next to their old silver Volvo station wagon and waving. For a minute I actually thought he was waving at me. I think I might've even lifted my hand to wave back at him. But then I noticed Jordan running down the other side of the steps to meet him. Naturally, she completely ignored me. Okay, maybe she didn't even see me. I realize how good I've been getting at making myself invisible. Jordan's dad gave her a big bear hug then ceremoniously opened the passenger door and, like a little princess, she just hopped in. It looked like they were going off to do something really great. I tried not to let myself think about that though. I have enough pain in my life without consciously inviting more.

I have a new habit now. I watch Dr. Bill every day after school. I hurry home and turn on the TV and pretend that he's really my dad. I feel quite proud of him as I watch him helping all these crazy, whacked-out people. Who knew there were so many nutcases in this country? Dr. Bill probably has guests lined up until 2073.

Then, during commercial breaks, I imagine Dr. Bill getting a milkshake with me, or teaching me to drive. I envision him taking me to the DMV to get my driver's license. I imagine him giving me a gold charm bracelet for my birthday and coming to my graduation. I can see him giving me away at my wedding, wiping a tear from his eye as he tells me I'm the prettiest girl in the world.

I know that other people would think I am totally nuts if they knew about my new Dr. Bill obsession, and I would never admit it to anyone, but for some reason it makes me feel a little bit better about my life.

fifteen

IT'S BEEN A TOTALLY CRUDDY DAY TODAY. AND IT DOESN'T HELP KNOWING that it's Jordan's birthday. Her sixteenth too! But, naturally, this has nothing to do with me. Why would I even imagine it would? Of course, I have NOT been invited by her or her family to participate in any birthday celebrations or activities. Even though I've always been there, smiling and singing to her, for the last ten years. I remember how Jordan always swore that she'd get her driver's license on her birthday. Well, I hope beyond hope that she fails big time today. I think I will cross my fingers all afternoon as I imagine her ramming her dad's Volvo right into the fire hydrant on Main Street. And I hope she gets that really mean driving-test lady, the one who dyes her hair a different color every week. I can just imagine that woman swearing at her as she leaps out of the car and gets soaking wet. That will show her.

I try to push my vindictive thoughts about Jordan from my mind as I go up the stairs to the apartment. I know that Dr. Bill would say that this kind of thinking is not healthy. As usual, no one's at home when I unlock the door. Bree has her soccer and Mom doesn't get off work until five. Normally, this absence of family spectators is a relief to me. It's my chance to sit down with Dr. Bill and just veg out for a couple of hours. But for some reason my home just feels lonelier than usual today.

Besides feeling lonely, I realize that I'm also hungry, which is rather interesting since I haven't had much of an appetite lately. But for some reason I feel absolutely ravenous today. Perhaps it's a sign that I'm finally getting over this whole stupid Jordan thing. I hope so.

Before turning on the TV, I head for the kitchen and start out, innocently enough, by quickly snarfing down the remnants of a bag of tortilla chips that were left sitting on the counter. Still not satisfied, I head for the refrigerator. I quickly concoct a sloppy peanut butter and jelly sandwich and pour a tall glass of milk. But in no time I have devoured these and *still* feel hungry.

I peel and eat a banana as I gaze blankly into the freezer compartment. Finally I spy what appears to be a carton of Goo Goo Cluster ice cream tucked way in the back. It is neatly hidden behind a bag of frozen peas. I'm fairly certain that this is the work of my greedy little sister. I retrieve the carton and open it up to find there's about a quarter of the sweet, sticky substance left. Then, instead of putting some in a bowl like a civilized person, I simply stick in a big spoon and head for the TV.

Mad at myself for missing the beginning of my favorite show, I flop down on the stone sofa and turn on the TV. Dr. Bill is talking to this really obese blonde. He looks really intense and as I eat my ice cream I lean forward to listen better. Today's topic is morbid obesity (that means you're fat enough to actually die from it, or perhaps from a side effect of it, I can't really remember). But all of his guests look like they weigh at least four or five hundred pounds. I wonder how they got there. Do they fly in a regular commercial airplane? Or do they have to make some kind of special arrangements to accommodate their size? I stare at these overly large people, mostly women, with a weird mix of pity and fascination. I am amazed that they would go on national television looking like that. But more than that, I wonder, how does a person actually let themselves go that far? Don't they ever look in the mirror?

"I eat when I'm sad," says the heavy blonde with the pretty blue eyes. Her pale arms are so flabby that they look like they're literally pouring out of her bright red tent dress.

"I eat when I'm lonely," says another heavy woman. She has short, dark hair and her face is so fat that I can't even make out her neck and chin. It's just like one big heap of flesh emerging from the neck of her blouse. Of course, she has facial features, but even those look unreal, as if they've been painted on. It's hard for me to imagine that there's a real live person living inside that enormous bulk of body.

"Food is my friend," she continues in a dead-serious voice. "It never lets me down. It never hurts or disappoints me."

"But it does make you fat," drawls Dr. Bill in that no-nonsense southern drawl that I've come to love.

"That's true," she says sadly.

"So, I gotta ask, how's that working for you?" he says. I smile at this question. It's a Dr. Bill favorite.

She shakes her head, causing the loose skin around her neck to jiggle like a warm bowl of tapioca pudding. "Not so well, I guess."

"So tell me, when did you first start putting on the weight?" he asks both of the women, speaking more gently now, like he's trying to ease the answer out of them. "I want you both to try to remember the specific time when food and weight first started becoming a real problem for you."

"It was back when I was a teenager," the blonde finally says. "I was really sad because my best friend had moved away, and I was so lonely that I just started to eat. I realize now that it was mostly sweets and carbohydrates. But it was so satisfying. Food just seemed to make my troubles melt away. It always made me feel—"

But before that woman can finish another sentence, I grab up the remote and turn off the TV. For a long time I sit staring at the blank TV screen and then I look down at the empty carton of ice cream still sitting in my lap. I feel slightly stunned as I consider my binge. And suddenly I want to gag myself and simply throw up. But I know enough about bulimia to realize that's not such a great idea either. *What is wrong with me?*

Totally disgusted with myself, I get up and head for the kitchen thinking that I'm probably going to turn out just like those poor women on Dr. Bill's show. Maybe I already have. I pause by the mirror near the front door, but I'm almost afraid to look. Finally I do, bracing myself.

But I look just the same as always. Same face, same hair, same hopeless expression.

"What in the world is wrong with you?" I demand as I stare at my pitiful image. I shake my finger in my face. "You better watch out, Kara!" But even as I'm looking I can imagine myself growing bigger and bigger. Just like that little girl who turns into a giant blueberry in *Willy Wonka and the Chocolate Factory.* I can see myself eating and eating until I look exactly like those ladies. And for the first time, I think I can really understand how things like that can actually happen to real people. And for the first time, I realize something like that could actually happen to me. It might already be happening! And the mere idea of it is chilling.

I throw away the empty ice-cream carton and go straight to my room. I quickly change into my sweats and running shoes, barely bothering to tie them properly. There's no time to waste. Okay, I realize there's nothing I can do about what I've already consumed, but at least I can try to work some of those calories off.

And yet I feel slow and sluggish and *fat* as I plod through town. I am jogging more than running now, and before long my bloated stomach begins to complain. I stop and simply walk for a while. Clutching my aching middle, I head for the park, seriously hoping that I'm not about to hurl. Not that I wouldn't mind losing all the crud that I consumed earlier. But the park is fairly crowded just now. There are kids playing soccer and people walking dogs and moms with little kids, and for whatever reason I just don't care to make a complete fool of myself today.

I go down to the duck pond and flop my out-of-shape self onto the cement bench. I try to breathe deeply, trying to calm my upset and overtaxed digestive system. I watch the ducks going in and out of the water. Some waddle over and peer curiously at me, hoping, I'm sure, that I might have some handouts for them. I feel ashamed to think of that bag of chips that I selfishly inhaled about an hour ago. I could've brought it down here to my little duck friends.

"Next time," I promise them. "I'll bring you something really good next time." I watch the big mallard, who keeps looking at me from the corner of his eye, almost like he's flirting with me. I think I'd like to give him a name. Maybe I'll call him Henry. Perhaps I'll name all of these ducks. I begin thinking of good names. I like the sound of Gladys and Orville and Gertrude for my fine feathered friends.

But then I realize that these ducks, like everyone else in the rest of the world, already have their own circle of friends. And, most likely, I wouldn't be welcome in their crowd either. I bend over and put my head in my hands, the defeated posture of a social wreck, a true reject, a total *loser.*

And I wonder if I will ever fit into life again.

sixteen

IT SEEMS LIKE EVERYONE AT SCHOOL IS OBSESSED WITH THE HARVEST Dance this year. It's at the end of the week and posters are plastered everywhere. I've heard through the grapevine that Jordan is going with Caleb Andrews. Caleb's a really good-looking junior who's part jock and part academic. I'm sure that Jordan must be feeling pretty pleased with herself right now.

I actually made a couple more feeble attempts to get Jeremy Thatcher's attention this week, but it's utterly hopeless. Maybe I should've focused my efforts on someone less inhibited than poor Jeremy. Now I'm afraid it's too late. Why I even want to go to this stupid dance is way beyond me. I think I must simply be a glutton for punishment. Or maybe it's just that the feeling of being left out of absolutely everything is really bumming me out.

As it turns out, even Amy and her motley group of friends have decided to go to the dance together.

"We're going to be crashers," says Amy with a twinkle in her eye. "We'll dress up really cool and come late and then just rock out until we've had enough. Then we'll split. It'll be cool."

"You mean you're not going to show up with your new college boyfriend?" teases Felicia at lunchtime on Thursday.

Amy narrows her eyes. "I told you, Leon doesn't know that I'm still *in* high school." She says this in a fairly uptight voice, and Felicia looks taken aback.

"How about you, Kara?" asks Felicia.

"Huh?" I look up from my current project. It's a watercolor painting that's not working out as well as I'd hoped. It's supposed to be a tree behind a pond, but it's looking more like a bush growing out of a mud puddle.

"She's asking if you're going to the dance," says Amy, as if she's a translator. Then she licks the tip of her drawing pencil and eyes me carefully. "So, are you?"

I shake my head and say, "Nah," then return my attention to rinsing out my paintbrush.

"Why not?" demands Amy.

I look up at her and vaguely wonder what the correct answer to her impertinent question is supposed to be. "I don't know," I shrug. "Probably because no one has asked me."

"You can go with us," Amy says quickly.

I try to imagine myself with Amy and her wild friends. I feel pretty sure they'll be getting high before "crashing" the dance. "Thanks," I tell her. "But that's okay."

"Too good for us?" she asks, lifting one eyebrow in that intimidating way of hers.

I shake my head. "That's not it. We're just different, you know. I'm sure you guys will have a really great time. But I just don't want to—"

"Why don't you go with me?" says Edgar. I think that's the first thing he's said today.

"Huh?" I look at him incredulously. Did he really just say what I think he said? Judging by his expression, he probably did. Still, I cannot for the life of me imagine going to a dance, or anywhere else for that matter, with Edgar Peebles. It's not that I'm a snob really. At least I hope not. But everyone has to draw their line somewhere.

"Why don't we go to the dance together, Kara?" he tries again. "It doesn't need to be like a real date. We could just go together. Sort of like Felicia and Aaron, you know?"

I stare at him and hope I don't look too horrified. "Oh, I don't know, Edgar. I don't really think—"

"Why not?" demands Amy. "You guys should just go and have fun."

"But I—"

"I know what you're thinking, Kara," says Amy as she suddenly stands up and goes over to where Edgar is sitting at the end of the table. "You're thinking what we're all thinking. You're thinking that Edgar is a geek." She pats him affectionately on the head. "Sorry, Edgar, but it's the truth."

He makes a funny face then just shrugs. "Yeah, I know."

I feel horrible for Edgar now. So much so that I almost feel like saying I'll go to the dance with him. But honestly, I can only push myself so far.

"All right," continues Amy, "so, we've established that Edgar is a geek. But we also know that he's a nice guy, right?"

"Right," echoes Felicia and I nod mutely.

"Okay." Amy is pacing now. She reminds me of a mad scientist. "The thing is, people, geekiness is only skin deep. It's just an image problem. And images are easily changed." She holds out her hands as if to make a point. "Look at me. Everyone used to think I was a pushover. I had mousy brown hair and no visible personality. And then one day I'd just had enough. I looked in the mirror and decided to reinvent myself." She snaps her fingers dramatically. "And, presto, here I am. Do you think anyone thinks I'm a pushover now?"

I just shake my head. If anything I would describe Amy as a bulldozer.

She nods. "See what I'm saying?"

"Not exactly," I say in a timid voice. All I can think is that I'd like to get out of here, but according to the clock we still have twenty minutes.

"Okay, what if I give Edgar here a makeover—"

"Wait a minute," says Edgar. "Do I have a vote in this?"

Amy gives him a playful shove. "Just chill for a minute."

"But you can't just force someone to have a makeover, Amy," says Felicia.

Amy frowns. "Why not?"

I laugh now. Leave it to Amy to believe she can get her way regardless of anything. "Amy," I say. "Edgar would probably feel ridiculous if you made him look like you and your friends. No offense, I think it really works for you. But Edgar is different."

"Well, I know *that,*" says Amy like she thinks I'm an idiot. "I wasn't going to make Edgar over to look like me or my friends. I was just going to make him look like Edgar, only the cool version."

"The cool version?" Now Edgar is looking interested.

"Yeah," says Amy with enthusiasm. "We'll cut your hair and get you some cool duds and you'll be a whole new guy."

Edgar seems to be considering this now and I'm feeling nervous. "But I don't—"

"I'll do it!" says Edgar with more enthusiasm than I've ever seen come from him. "I've been asking God to do something to change me," he continues eagerly. "I've been praying to become the kind of guy that other people will listen to."

"See!" Amy points her finger triumphantly at him. "God must work in mysterious ways!"

"I guess so," says Edgar. "Do you really think you can do this?" Amy nods then she turns to me. "So, Kara, are you in?"

"In?"

"Yeah, if I can make over Edgar so that he's not a geek, will you go to the dance with him?"

I don't know what to say. Either answer, yes or no, would be open for misinterpretation. "I don't know . . ."

"Come on, Kara, be a sport," says Felicia. "If Edgar is willing to have a makeover, you should be willing to go to the dance with him."

"Besides," says Amy, "what do you have to lose? Your best friend dumped you for a bunch of shallow social climbers anyway. Do you want to be like her?"

"But it's so —"

"Here's the deal," says Amy suddenly. "How about if I give Edgar the makeover and if you see him and are still worried about going to the dance, then you don't have to. Okay?"

"Well . . ."

"And I'll do it tonight so that you can see him tomorrow," she offers. "You don't even have to decide until then. Okay?"

Now I'm thinking that's probably a safe agreement. Chances are I won't have to go out with Edgar at all. "Okay," I say with some reservation.

"Really?" says Edgar with hopeful eyes.

I feel like I'm going to be sick. "Really," I say in a flat voice. What am I getting myself into? Maybe I really will be sick tomorrow.

"If you don't like how Edgar looks, you don't have to go," promises Amy. Then she grabs Edgar by both hands and makes him stand up. She looks at him then laughs. "This is gonna be fun!"

Poor Edgar! I'm thinking as I finally leave the art room and head for my next class. What am I thinking? *Poor me!* And what on earth have I gotten myself into? I can just imagine Jordan's reaction when she sees me at the dance with Edgar Peebles.

But by the end of the day, I'm thinking maybe it wouldn't be such a bad thing, really. I'm thinking that it might be worth going out with Edgar for no other reason than to put myself right in Jordan Ferguson's snooty face. Suddenly I can imagine myself at the dance with Edgar, Class Geek. I can see us walking right up to Jordan and Caleb and I would say something like, "Hey, Jordan, I like your dress. Did Abbie help you pick it out? How's your mom doing anyway? Did your dad ever finish restoring that Harley yet? Make sure you tell Leah hi for me. I saw her at the grocery store last week and I just love what she's done with her hair." Oh, I could go on and on, and Jordan would be stuck standing there with her *ex*-best friend and the geek. Or maybe we'd just be the geek couple. Oh, I'm thinking it might be absolutely divine. If only I could work up the nerve.

But by Friday morning I am feeling seriously worried. I don't think there's any way I can pull this off. I know it will hurt Edgar's feelings to back out of this. But then he's such a nice guy, and a Christian to boot. I'm sure he'll forgive me in time.

I go into art class with a speech all prepared. I'll say that it's not him, it's me, that I'm just not ready to do anything that "social" yet. Maybe later in the year. And then I see him. Or at least I think it's him. I'm not entirely sure. A number of kids are already standing around him and Amy looks like that proverbial cat who swallowed the canary.

"Kara," she calls out in a sing-song voice. "Come here."

I slowly walk over to where the group is clustered around (is it really?) Edgar. His red hair is cut short and slightly choppy and the ends have been darkened to a shade about the color of mahogany. He has on a dark plum-colored shirt that is totally un-Edgar like, in fact it looks retro, but the most surprising change is with his glasses. Instead of his usual lopsided silver wire rims, he now has on a pair of black-framed glasses that remind me of Buddy Holly, or at least the guy who played him in that old TV movie I saw just last week.

"Wow," I say as I get closer to him. "You look amazingly cool, Edgar."

"So, you'll go to the dance with me?"

I look from Edgar to Felicia, who seems to be in complete shock over this transformation, and then to Amy, who is grinning like a drunk monkey.

"I think I need a makeover now," I tell them.

This makes everyone laugh.

"I can take care of that," says Amy.

I turn back to her and take a good look at her dark dyed hair and outlined eyes and then cringe. "I'm just kidding," I say quickly.

"I'm not." She peers at me like she's looking at a blank canvas now. "There's no way you're going out with Edgar looking like *that.*"

Well, I must admit I've let myself go in the past few weeks, but that comment does seem a bit harsh. "But I—"

"No buts," says Amy firmly.

And so it is that I find myself giving Amy my address and she is telling me that she'll come by right after school. "Do you have any money, Kara?"

I frown at her. "You mean you charge for—"

"No." Although she seems to consider this. "That's not a bad idea, but I meant do you have any money in case we need to get you something?"

"I have a little babysitting money, but not enough—"

"You'd be surprised at the bargains you can find at Salvation Army," she says without batting an eyelash.

"Salvation Army?" I wonder if she's serious.

"Oh, yeah, it's the best place to get really cool stuff. That's where Edgar and I went yesterday."

"Did you get his glasses there?"

She laughs. "No, those were a pair of his dad's old glasses that have the same prescription as Edgar's. He just uses them as spares. But I saw them on his dresser and thought they looked pretty cool."

I nod. "Yeah, they did. You're actually pretty good at this, Amy."

"I know. I think I might have to become a designer or something."

I think Amy might be the most confident person I know. Well, at least in my age group. Lots of grownups *appear* to have confidence, although it might be just an act, it's hard to know. But Amy is one of those girls who seems totally unflappable. I mean, she can get pretty mad and lose her temper and stuff. But it's like no one ever really gets under her skin. Even when other kids (like Jordan's crowd, for instance) pick on her or make fun of her weird clothes or whatever, she just seems to handle it better than anyone I know. Oh, sure, she might use some foul language or hand gestures, but it's like she just doesn't let it get to her. I find that impressive.

It's not that I'm ready to become best friends with Amy. For one thing, I doubt that she'd even be interested in someone like me. And, besides that, I don't really want to get involved in her particular kind of lifestyle. But at the same time, I wouldn't mind getting to know her better. Now it looks like I will.

seventeen

MOM AND BREE ARE LOOKING AT ME LIKE I'VE LOST MY MIND WHEN AMY and I walk into the apartment with our Salvation Army bags. They haven't met Amy before, and I suppose she's not exactly the kind of friend they're used to seeing with me.

"What's up?" asks Mom. I can tell by the sound of her voice that she's trying to act like, "Hey, I'm cool. I can handle this." Parents can be so clueless sometimes.

So I quickly introduce Amy to my tiny family and start to head for my room.

"We're doing a makeover on Kara," Amy explains to them, pushing a strand of hair out of her eyes, which reveals the dragon tattoo she sports on her wrist. I can tell she's oblivious to their amusement at her slightly unconventional appearance.

"That's, uh, nice," says my mom, but I can tell by her tone that she's not entirely convinced. In fact, I'm sure she's feeling pretty worried right now. But that's okay.

"This way," I say as I lead Amy to my room. I can hear Bree suppressing giggles as I close the door behind us.

"Do you *really* know what you're doing?" I ask her as I set my bag on the bed. I've already made it perfectly clear that we are *not* going to cut *or* dye my hair. It's one of the few things about myself that I still actually like.

"Just chill," she tells me for the umpteenth time. Then she begins pulling stuff from the bags.

Meanwhile, I sit down on my bed and just watch her. Her jet-black hair, her strange layers of dark clothing, her tattoos and numerous piercings are starting to make me feel nervous. I am such a fool for getting myself into this. What was I thinking?

"This is so cool," she says as she holds up a dress straight out of the sixties. "I can't believe no one snatched up this little gem already."

"I can." I frown at the minidress in her hands. The fabric looks like an unfortunate explosion of black and orange daisies.

"But it looked so good on you at the store," says Amy. "Of course, it'll look better when we get you finished."

Soon she has me dressed in the minidress, black fishnets, and these knee-high black boots that are made out of some kind of shiny plastic material that I'm sure won't be able to breathe. Not that breathing is a prerequisite here.

"Now for your hair and makeup." She points to the chair at my desk. "Sit down."

I know by the look in her eyes that there's no use in arguing with her now, so, feeling like I'll soon be the "fashion don't" example in *Mademoiselle*, I obediently sit down and stare at my legs. The black strings from the fishnet stockings are beginning to imprint neat little Xs across my knees. It's actually sort of interesting looking.

"Hold your head up," she tells me as she brushes then back-combs and styles my hair. I can't imagine what it's going to look like. But finally she seems to be done.

Then she clips some big black hoop earrings onto my ears and slips several large chunky bracelets on my wrist. I think they're all made of plastic. Plastic must've been big in the sixties.

"You can't look yet," she warns me. "We've got to do your makeup."

I look at Amy's dramatic eye makeup and think maybe this is where I should draw the line. "Oh, I don't—"

"Hey, this is *my* makeover," she tells me with narrowed eyes. "Don't start freaking now."

So I continue to submit, preparing myself for the worst. Finally, she steps back and I can tell she's done. She's glancing at her watch now and looking a little nervous. This is *not* reassuring.

"Okay, I guess you can look now."

I stand up and slowly walk over to where the full-length mirror hangs on my closet door. Bracing myself, I look. And then I look again. Then I begin to laugh.

"What's wrong?" she demands.

"Who is *that?*" I finally say.

"It's *psychedelic Kara.*" Amy's snickering now.

I study the whole outfit and am surprised that I don't hate it. In fact, it's kind of interesting in a weird, slightly theatrical way. "Tell me the truth, Amy, do you think I look ridiculous?"

"No way. I think you look hot. I'm actually kind of jealous that I didn't keep that outfit for myself."

I stare at the image in the mirror again. Part of my hair is piled high on my head and the rest is down my back. The makeup is more than I would normally wear, but it seems to go with the outfit, and I think I like the pale lipstick.

"So," she looks impatient now. "What do you think?"

"It's really different, but I actually kind of like it."

"*Kind of?*" She looks mad now. "Listen, Kara, I think you look really hot. In fact, I'm getting worried that I spent so much time here that I might not have time to fix myself up. And now you're saying that you only *kind of like*—"

"Okay," I tell her. "I *like* it. I really do, Amy. You did a fantastic job. Thanks so much!" I look at the clock by my bed. "And I hope you still have enough time to get ready. Didn't you say you guys were going late anyway?"

"Yeah, I'll be fine." She studies me now. "So, really, do you like it?"

I nod. "I never would've done something like this myself. But I *really* do like it. And the makeup is fun. It really looks like the sixties. I feel like I just stepped out of an old movie."

She smiles. "Good. It was fun doing it."

"You really could do this for a living," I tell her as she gathers up her backpack and stuff. "I feel like I should pay you or something."

"Nah. You and Edgar were just my guinea pigs. Someday I'll get really good at this and then I'll start charging." She laughs. "And then you can say, 'I knew her when . . .'"

I thank her again as we walk to the front door.

"Oh, my word!" Mom is staring from the kitchen now. The freezer is wide open and she's got a bag of frozen corn dangling from one hand. But she looks totally shocked.

"What do you think?" asks Amy. She pauses by the front door and waits for my mom's reaction.

My mom shoves the corn in the freezer then covers her mouth with her hand, but I can tell she's smiling. "Oh, Kara, you look adorable."

"Adorable?" I frown at the sound of that, but Amy just laughs.

"Okay, that's the wrong word. You look very cool, Kara. Now, turn around so I can see you better."

So I do a little spin. "Isn't Amy talented?"

Mom nods. "She sure is. Good work, Amy."

"Thanks, it was fun. But I gotta split."

My mom is still staring at me after Amy leaves. Only now she has this kind of dreamy look. "Kara, did you know that I used to dress like that? Honestly, I had a dress almost exactly like that in junior high?"

"Really? I actually thought it was kind of ugly at first. Like revenge of the daisies."

"Well, that's the sixties for you." Mom takes a loaf of bread out of a grocery bag. "It was like a mix of ugly and cute. But I think you look cute. But what are you planning to do all dressed up like that?"

"I guess I'm going to the Harvest Dance."

"You *guess?*"

"Well, this kid in art, Edgar Peebles, invited me to go with him. We're just friends though, and he's really sort of a geek. Although he's looking a lot better since Amy gave him a—"

"Kara!" squeals Bree as she emerges from her room. "Look at you!"

I hold out my arms and attempt to walk like a runway model through the living room. "What do you think?" I ask as I tilt my chin up.

"I think you look totally cool. Can I borrow that outfit sometime?"

I shrug. "We'll see."

"Kara's going to the Harvest Dance," Mom announces as she returns to putting groceries away. I can tell that she's happy I'm going out. I'm sure she's probably been concerned about my mental health lately.

"We should take her picture before she leaves," suggests Bree.

"Good idea." Now Mom runs off in search of her camera and I am subjected to an impromptu photo session, but it's not really so bad.

I start getting nervous as the time draws near for Edgar to pick me up. I don't even know whether he drives or not. I think he's a junior, but somehow he's always seemed younger to me. I wonder if his parents will have to drive us tonight. I imagine this frumpy middle-aged couple driving up in a white Dodge minivan. It probably has all those religious sort of bumper stickers on it. The plan was to go out for dinner before the dance, because, according to Felicia, that is what people do. Still, I'm wishing I had only agreed to go to the dance. I imagine Edgar and me eating some really lame dinner, probably at Nate's Chuck Wagon where you get your food cafeteria style. Meanwhile, his parents would be waiting for us out in the minivan. Maybe they'll be reading their Bibles or listening to religious music. Or, here's a scary thought, maybe they will join us for dinner. I can just see the four of us at the Chuck Wagon. Oh, crud, why did I ever agree to this in the first place?

But suddenly Edgar is here and I quickly introduce him to Mom. Fortunately, Bree has already left with her friend Sunny to see a movie—a relief since I don't really need her making any stupid geek comments about Edgar once this evening is over, which I'm hoping will be soon. And naturally, I know that going out with Edgar will be a one-time thing.

We go downstairs and there, parked in front of the apartment complex, is an old black Cadillac. "Sorry about the wheels," he apologizes. "I borrowed it from my uncle."

I'm just relieved that it's not the white minivan being driven by the Bible-toting Mr. and Mrs. Peebles. "Hey, it's fine," I assure him. "It sort of goes with my outfit."

He nods. "Yeah, we're like a flash from the past." Then he gets more serious. "But I should tell you that I think you look really good, Kara. I like your outfit."

"Compliments of Amy," I say as he opens the door for me. "A Weatherspoon original."

"You know, she'll probably be a famous designer someday."

"That's what she's hoping." I look around the ancient car. I can tell that someone has tried to clean it up, but it reeks with the musty smell of cigarette smoke, which is only slightly masked by the bright green pine tree hanging from the mirror. Still, I don't mind so much. It's way better than the minivan scenario.

Edgar drives us to the other side of town, parking in front of a little café called The Blue Moon. Now I've seen this place before, just in passing, but I've never gone in. I hear jazz music as we go inside, and I notice right off that it's kind of funky looking with its black-and-white checkerboard floor and old-fashioned booths. And as I read the handwritten menu, I notice that the prices are pretty reasonable. A relief since I came prepared to buy my own dinner tonight. I don't want Edgar thinking this is an actual date. I finally decide on the lemon chicken. I'm not even sure why, since I've never had it before. Probably just because it is the cheapest thing next to a hamburger basket, which I think would be rather tacky tonight.

"I didn't get you a corsage or anything," Edgar apologizes after we've placed our orders. "I just wasn't sure what the proper protocol was, you know. I mean I haven't really done anything like this before."

I can tell he's embarrassed and I wave my hand. "Hey, don't worry. Actually, I'm glad you didn't. This outfit isn't exactly the corsage type anyway. Besides, this isn't supposed to be like a *real* date, remember? We're just supposed to be a couple of friends going to the dance together."

He smiles with what seems relief. "Yeah, that makes it more fun, doesn't it? Less pressure."

We manage to make small talk during dinner, mostly about

chess. I tell him that I can play a little but can't imagine playing in a real chess tournament. I don't mention that most people think it's slightly geeky. I have a feeling he knows this. But then he tries to explain some simple chess tricks to me by drawing a diagram on the paper napkin. I nod and pretend to understand then I stuff the messy napkin into my purse like I plan to study it later. Not.

Finally the waitress brings our bill, but when I offer to pay for my portion, Edgar refuses. "I know this isn't really a date," he says, "but I'd like to pay if you don't mind. And don't worry, I won't act like you owe me anything, Kara."

"Okay," I agree, "if it makes you feel better."

He smiles. "It does."

Now I must say that when Edgar smiles, his whole face lights up and he's actually rather cute. In fact, I'm thinking with Edgar's recent makeover he's quite good-looking. Okay, maybe I'm imagining this. But it's possible. It's also possible that we'll make quite a striking couple at the dance tonight. And suddenly I'm envisioning myself in the old Cinderella role. The poor, abused stepsister (or cast-off friend) shows up at the dance and just blows everyone away. It could happen.

Now Edgar's driving back toward the school, and suddenly it feels like my dinner has sprung to life and is dancing the Funky Chicken in my stomach. I reassure myself that it's just my stupid nerves, and I seriously try to relax. I breathe deeply and stare blankly at the pine tree dangling from the mirror. *I can do this,* I assure myself. *Everything's going to be perfectly fine.*

Just the same, I wonder why on earth I wanted to put myself through something like this tonight. I mean, hasn't my life been bad enough without adding this completely new form of torture to it? But, on the other hand, I think, *Hey, why not?* Why shouldn't I do something wild and crazy for a change? Something totally out of the norm. It could be a brand-new beginning for me. Maybe even for Edgar too.

And suddenly, I feel slightly hopeful. It's like I'm thinking tonight might be some kind of a liberation for me. Like a coming-out party, whatever that's supposed to be. I imagine that I, Kara Hendricks, am announcing to the world, or at least to Jackson High School, that I no longer give a flying fig what other people think of me anymore. It will be my way of showing Jordan Ferguson and all her superficial friends that I, too, can have a life. I, too, can have friends. Okay, they might not be the kind of friends that Jordan would choose. But who knows? Mine might be a whole lot more interesting.

However, I do have one predominate concern right now: I really, really hope that Edgar knows how to dance. I never thought to ask him about this little detail before. And I'm not terribly reassured by the fact that he comes from a churchy sort of background that may not encourage dancing. But somehow, the idea of sitting on the side-lines all night long, like a couple of stuck-in-the-sixties wallflower geeks, just will *not* work for me tonight. *I really need to dance.*

eighteen

EDGAR AMAZINGLY FINDS A PARKING SPACE AND PARKS THE LONG, BLACK Caddie near the entrance. I think this might be a good sign. Imagining I am *Someone*, I wait for Edgar to come around and open the door for me. I've already figured out that this guy likes playing the gentleman. Then I leisurely step out, extending one black-booted leg and then the next. I notice some kids across the street looking at us like they're wondering who we are. And I really feel like maybe we are celebrities.

When we go into the dance, I realize that we probably should've stretched out our dinner longer and made a fashionably late appearance. I assume that's what Jordan and her friends will be doing since they're not here yet. Amy and her gang aren't here yet either, but that was their plan. I should've taken the hint. I don't even see Felicia and the Rubensteins. But maybe this is a good thing. It gives Edgar and me a chance to get ourselves somewhat acclimated.

"Do you want something to drink?" he asks, glancing over his shoulder as if he's expecting to be pounced on by someone. Maybe that's happened before. Who knows what life is like for someone like Edgar Peebles?

"Sure," I tell him, and together we walk over to the refreshment table to get some punch. We slowly consume the sweet orange concoction as we watch what few couples are dancing. Then to my surprise, Edgar invites me to dance.

"Sure," I say, suppressing the urge to inquire, "Do you really know how to dance?"

As it turns out, he's not half bad. And now I'm thinking this time might come in handy for us. Get the kinks out before anyone who matters shows up to see us fumbling around like amateurs.

Before long, I realize that I'm actually having fun. And smiling and even laughing. It's been a long time since I've felt this happy, and I must admit it feels strange. Felicia and Jessie are here with their dates now, and we pause to chat with them.

"You guys look absolutely fantastic," says Jessie Rubenstein as if she really means it.

"Amy Weatherspoon gave them makeovers," explains Felicia.

"She's good." Jessie gives us her nod of approval as their four-some goes out to the dance floor.

Then, as Edgar and I pause for a little break, I notice a large group of kids coming in. I can hear them from here, and I suspect that it's Jordan's new circle of friends. You can tell who they are just by the way they walk and talk and throw their heads back to laugh and basically act like they own the whole place. Every single one of them just seems to ooze confidence. I can feel my stomach begin-ning to tighten again, but I remind myself to just relax and breathe. Everything will be okay.

I can see Jordan now. She's wearing a pale green dress that looks like it's straight out of the fifties. Now I notice that the other girls are wearing what appear to be fifties dresses too. All in a rainbow of pas-tel colors—pink and blue and lavender. It's obvious that they planned it. They also have matching purses and shoes and all of them are wearing wrist corsages. I tell myself that they look like a bunch of prissy dorks, but I know that they actually look pretty cool. And I realize how out of place my sixties outfit would look among them.

They're walking right past us now. I feel their curious glances, but I can't tell what's behind them. Do they recognize us? Do they care? Are they impressed by our unique fashion statement? I stand up straighter and square my shoulders as I turn my attention back to Edgar and smile as if he's just said something wonderfully funny.

When I glance their way again, I catch Jordan looking directly at me. Her expression is one of wonder and disbelief. But once again, I can't exactly read it. Does she think I look cool or ridiculous? Will she say anything? I remember how it wasn't that long ago that Jordan really liked sixties fashions. Based on that, I'm guessing that she would probably approve of this outfit. Maybe it's just Edgar she can't figure out. She probably doesn't even know who he is. Well, that's fine. Give her something to think about.

Soon we go back to the dance floor and I try to keep an eye on Jordan and Caleb without being too obvious. I have to admit, if only to myself, they do make an attractive couple. Still, I don't want her to see me spying, so I attempt to direct my attention back to Edgar.

"Look who just got here," he says in a quiet voice, as he nods toward the door.

I look to see a throng of dark clothing swaggering into the cafeteria. "Amy's group."

"Yeah, they look like a motorcycle gang."

I laugh. "Amy probably gave them all makeovers."

Soon Amy and her friends are out on the floor and the noise and activity level seem to immediately increase. I'm guessing by their expressions that some of them are high or drunk or both. Including Amy. In fact, when I say "hey" to her, she's so spaced out that she doesn't even seem to know me.

"You okay?" I ask her.

"Huh?" She looks at me with blurry eyes, then slowly nods as if it's all coming back to her.

"*Kara!*" she exclaims in a slurred voice. "You look sh-plashing. I mean sh-mashing." Then she begins to giggle and goes back to dancing with a tall dark-haired guy.

"I hope she's okay," I say to Edgar. "She looks pretty wasted, don't you think?"

He just shrugs. "Doesn't look like much fun if you ask me."

Suddenly I see Amy staggering straight toward me with a wild look on her face. "I need — the bathroom," she says urgently.

So leaving poor Edgar by himself on the dance floor, I grab Amy by the arm and direct her toward the girls' restroom.

"Are you going to throw up?" I ask as we hurry toward the door.

"Yeah, I think so." She is pressing her hand over her mouth now. Not a good sign.

Naturally, there's a clog of pastel dresses blocking the way as Jordan's friends gather in front of the mirror to touch up their lipstick and powder their noses. "Make way," I yell as I attempt to press through the chiffon rainbow. But they are not listening. "Hey, we've got a sick girl here and she's — "

But it's too late. Amy is already starting to hurl. Man, I've never seen girls in dresses and heels move so fast. Most of them escape in time, but Amy does manage to hit the hemline of Betsy Mosler's pale pink dress and satin shoes with a spray of chunky yellow barf. Not a pretty picture. I notice that some of it has even landed on my shiny black boots. At least they should clean more easily.

"Gross!" screams Betsy as she stares in horror at her ruined dress and shoes. Then she lets loose with a stream of cuss words that could make a biker blush. "You are so sick, Amy Weatherspoon!"

"Yeah," I quickly agree as I direct Amy into an empty stall, hoping she'll manage to hit the toilet this time. "She *is* sick. I tried to warn you guys."

"You should've taken her out to the street," screams Betsy, no less than hysterical now. "That's where dogs like her belong."

Fortunately, I don't think Amy can hear this cruel comment since she's puking her guts into the toilet just now. I stand behind her and help her to balance as I hold onto her jet-black hair so that it doesn't get into the stinky mess. I keep thinking she should be done by now, but she seems to go on and on. I wonder what she had for dinner, or was it just alcohol? Then I worry that she might actually need medical attention. I've heard of kids dying from alcohol poisoning. But finally she seems to recover. She is breathing hard as she slowly stands up, hanging to the side walls for support. She looks at me with watery eyes that have created two black streaks down her cheeks. She grabs up a wad of toilet paper and attempts to wipe off her mouth and face and hands. I try to help clean off the black streaks.

"Thanks," she mutters in a hoarse voice.

"Sure. Are you okay?"

She sighs. "I guess so."

Still in the stall, I turn around to see that several of the girls remain clustered in the bathroom. Hovering, like faithful drones as they attend to the Queen Bee, they use wet paper towels to clean Betsy's dress and shoes. She certainly seems to be getting plenty of miles out of her poor-victim routine. I am relieved that Jordan is not among them.

But Betsy pauses from this activity to glare at us when we step out into full view. "People like you should not be allowed to live on this earth," she sputters, "let alone attend school dances. You're both totally disgusting."

I roll my eyes at her and help Amy get to the sink, where she bends down to wash her hands and face in cold water. I take a moment to wipe some of the muck off of my boots.

"What's the matter?" asks Betsy in a mocking tone. "Did you get some of that on yourself? Pretty nasty, isn't it?"

I turn and look Betsy in the eye now. "Look, it's not like Amy did it on purpose, you know. And if you hadn't noticed, it's not like she's having a real great time tonight either."

"Then why don't you losers just clear out of here?" Betsy seethes. "It's not like anyone *wants* you around here anyway. Freaks like you aren't welcome at this dance."

I return her stare. "Despite *popular* opinion, it's still a free country, Betsy. And Amy and I can come to this dance if we want to. Although, why we'd want to when people like you try to spoil it for everyone just beats the heck outta me."

Now Betsy's looking at me with narrowed eyes, as if she thinks I'm crazy. She turns her head slightly, as if talking only to her friends and says, "I *cannot*, for the life of me, understand how Jordan Ferguson could ever have been friends with someone like *that*. Man, it's no wonder that Jordan can't stand this loser anymore."

The other girls laugh. Except for Ashley Crow, although her expression is a hard-to-read mix of disgust and I think boredom. But I decide I don't care as I lead Amy out of the bathroom, which now smells like a bad mixture of puke and designer perfume. And frankly I'm not even sure which one smells worse.

"I'm going to find Edgar and go home," I tell Amy. "You need a ride?"

"You're going home?" she says with surprise. "But the party just began."

I look at her incredulously. "You actually want to stay here? After all that?"

She shrugs. "Sure, why not?"

I just shake my head. "Yeah, well, whatever. Have a good time."

Then she pauses and puts a hand on my shoulder. "Thanks, Kara."

I attempt to smile at her. "Sure, anytime." Then thinking better of it, I add, "But you'd probably feel better if you laid off that crud, Amy. It can't be good for you."

She just laughs. "Hard to say. Maybe it is. Maybe it's not."

On my way to find Edgar, I hope that he won't be too disappointed to leave early. But if he is, I will simply offer to walk home by myself. No big deal, since it's only a few blocks anyway.

"Kara?"

I stop to see Jordan looking at me like she wants to say something. "Huh?"

"I wanted to talk to you for a minute, Kara."

I shrug. "Sure, whatever."

Then she motions for me to follow her over to a dimly lit corner. If I didn't know better, I'd think she was trying to score some kind of a drug deal. But like her faithful old shadow, following her beck and call, I obediently go.

Suddenly it occurs to me that this could turn into something even more shocking than a drug deal. Maybe she overheard Betsy laying into me and feels sorry. And maybe she wants to apologize for all that's gone on this fall. I wonder if she wants to beg me to come back into her life. To plead with me to return to being her best friend, just like before.

Even so, I remind myself, I don't want to make it too easy for her. And after everything that's gone on just now, that whole crazy scene in the restroom, I suppose my patience has worn a little thin tonight.

"Well, I know it's probably been kind of hard on you lately since we're not, uh, well, we're not such good friends anymore."

"Not such good friends?" I look at her as if she's lost her marbles. "Jordan, if you haven't noticed, we're not friends at all. What exactly are you trying to say here?"

"Well, okay, I guess we're not really friends anymore. But we used to be."

I laugh. "I'm surprised you'd admit that in public." Then I look around. "Although I guess no one else can hear this, can they?"

"And that's for your own good, Kara. I only asked to talk to you to let you know that I'm concerned about you."

"You're concerned about me?" I feel my voice get a little louder now, but I don't think I care.

"Yes, you're hanging with some questionable people and—"

"Questionable people?"

"Yes. Like Amy Weatherspoon, for instance. Everyone knows that girl is nothing but trouble."

"Hey, Amy may have her problems, but at least she's a good friend. Not like some people I used to know."

Now Jordan scowls. "I don't know why I'm even wasting my time trying to talk to you, Kara."

"I don't know either, Jordan. And I'm sure your friends won't like it. Betsy already told me what you think of me." I put my hands on my hips now and look her straight in the eyes. "Not that I care."

"Well, fine, Kara. Go ahead and make a mess of your life and act like a total fool. What do I care anyway?"

I shake my head now. "Oh, you do care, Jordan. Because I used to be your best friend and I have the power to make you look bad."

She frowns now, but says nothing.

"Not that I'd trouble myself to do that," I say quickly. "Because I think your new friends are already doing a great job of it themselves." Then I turn and walk away. It helps that I'm wearing these tall, black boots. It's like they're putting this authority into my step. But just the same, I can feel hot tears burning in my eyes. And I want to hurry up and find Edgar before they actually spill out and make black streaks down my cheeks like I just witnessed with Amy.

Edgar is no more eager to stay than I am. But I'm not sure whether to be disappointed or relieved. I was sort of hoping that I could just walk home by myself. I don't really want to have to explain this whole thing to anyone right now. Of course, it does occur to me that I'll probably have to explain it to Mom.

"You want to go get some dessert or something?" he asks after we're back in the long, black Caddie.

I slump down into the seat and wish I could simply vanish into the musty upholstery.

"You okay, Kara?"

I just shrug.

"You want to talk about it?"

I turn and look at him. And something about that sweet yet intense expression in his eyes lures me in.

I nod.

He puts the car into gear and heads toward town.

Now I'm thinking that perhaps someone like Edgar can really understand how it feels to be spurned and rejected and betrayed by an ex-best friend. Or not. Come to think of it, Edgar doesn't exactly seem like the kind of guy who's had a whole lot of experience with best friends or even friends in general.

Well, it just stands to reason that I'd come to something like this before too long. And all in one night too. First I get barfed on by the school bad girl, and then I get dissed by the school popular girl. And now I am ready to spill my guts to the school nerd. It just figures.

nineteen

WE GO TO A SLEEPY LITTLE COFFEE SHOP ON MAIN STREET, WHICH IS just as well since I know it's unlikely we'll see any kids from school here. This is the kind of place where old people hang out and eat coconut cream pie and glazed donuts as they read the newspaper or talk about the weather or politics or whatever it is that old people talk about these days.

We sit at a table by the window and order coffee, which tastes metallic and bitter. Even when I doctor it up with sugar and cream, it's still pretty disgusting.

"I don't really like coffee," I confess.

He laughs. "Well, even though I drink coffee, I have to admit this is some pretty nasty stuff."

And so we both order milkshakes. I push my coffee to the side and watch as he takes small sips from his chipped cup. Who would've figured that Edgar Peebles was a coffee drinker?

"Sorry, I'm such a hopeless date," I say in a quiet voice. Actually, I'm thankful that I managed to keep from crying on the way here.

"Hey, you're fine. I'm probably the hopeless one."

I shake my head. "No. You were great, Edgar. I was actually having fun. Until . . . "

"Did something happen in the bathroom?" he asks. "I mean

when Amy got sick."

"Sort of." I pause as the middle-aged waitress sets our milk-shakes on the table. They're those old-fashioned kind where they bring the stainless steel container with extra in it. I haven't had one of these in ages.

We both taste our shakes. Mine is chocolate and better than I expected. Edgar ordered peanut butter, of all things. I never even knew there was such a thing as peanut butter milkshakes.

"How is it?" I ask.

He grins. "Superb. Ya wanna taste?"

So I take a spoonful and am surprised to discover that it's really good. "I'll have to have one of those next time I'm here," I tell him.

"So what happened?" asked Edgar.

I briefly described the barfing-in-the-bathroom scene, which simply made him laugh. "Betsy got what she deserved," he said. But then he frowned. "Still, I don't see why that should be so upsetting."

"It wasn't just that. I ran into Jordan on the way out and she attempted to give me this little lecture on how to act. Like she was afraid I was going to embarrass her or something. I actually thought that maybe she was going to apologize and that she maybe wanted to be friends again." Okay, that last line does it to me. Now I am starting to cry. I stare down at my milkshake and feel like a total moron. "Sorry," I manage to say as I wipe my nose with the stiff paper napkin.

"Hey, it's okay. I understand. If it makes you feel any better I've been hurt a few times too."

I look up at him. "Did you ever lose a best friend?"

"As a matter of fact, I did." He frowns now and I'm not sure if he wants to go into any detail, but finally he does. "I was in sixth grade. Tommy Benson and I had been best friends since third grade. We were both the smart kids in the class, you know, the eggheads, book-worms, nerds, geeks, whatever the fashionable term at the time was."

I nod sadly. "Yeah, I've probably used those terms a few times myself. Sorry."

"It's okay. Everyone does occasionally. But anyway, something happened that year, and Tommy's mom said we couldn't spend time together anymore."

"That's not fair. Parents shouldn't be able to tell you who you can or can't be friends with."

"As it turned out, we ended up moving that summer anyway. But I was really sad to lose Tommy as my friend. I guess I haven't really had anyone I'd call a best friend since then. Well, other than one." He looks up and smiles now.

"Who's that?"

"Jesus."

I sigh. "Oh, yeah, I almost forgot about that."

"But it's really true. Jesus became my best friend and he's better than any human friend. He never lets me down."

I'm sure my expression is one of pretty strong skepticism.

"Hey, I'm not trying to preach at you, Kara. I'm just saying the truth. Jesus really is my best friend. Without him, I'm not sure what I'd do to survive. But it wouldn't be pretty."

I fiddle with my long spoon now. "Must be nice to grow up in a religious family," I say absently.

But this just makes him laugh. "Are you kidding?"

I look up at him, feeling slightly confused. "No, not exactly. Why is that so funny?"

"My family isn't exactly religious, Kara."

"Oh. I just assumed . . ."

"Well, you know what they say about *that* word."

"So, your family doesn't go to church then?"

"First of all, my family is mainly just my dad and me these days. And my dad never goes to church. Fact is, he's an alcoholic."

"That's too bad."

"Not really. He's a recovering alcoholic. Last count he hadn't had a drink in eight months and about seventeen days."

"Good for him. But what happened to your mom?"

"My parents divorced several years ago."

"Was it because of your dad's drinking problem?"

"No, it was because they couldn't be together anymore."

"Why not?"

Now Edgar is looking at me, really studying me, as if he's trying to determine what I'm made of. *Good question,* I'm thinking. *I wonder if he can figure it out.*

"My parents couldn't be together because my mom is serving time."

"Serving time?"

"Yeah. In prison. She was convicted on drug charges and is doing ten to twelve years in the state pen."

"Oh." I wonder if my surprise shows in my face.

"Yeah, I don't usually tell anyone. But I thought maybe you could handle it. You seem like a mature person to me."

"Thanks."

"Yeah, that's the reason Tommy and I couldn't be friends anymore. His mom was worried that my family was a bad influence. As it turns out, she was right."

"But you're not a bad influence."

He shrugs. "That's only because of God's influence on me."

"So your mom's in prison and your dad's an alcoholic. Go figure."

"Recovering alcoholic," he corrects. "In fact, he had an AA meeting tonight."

"Well, good for him."

Now the conversation comes to a lull and I feel the need to divulge some family secrets, just to balance things out.

"Well, my parents are divorced too," I tell him.

He nods as if he already knew that.

"My mom is pretty ordinary. Just a hard-working single mom. I'm not sure why she hasn't remarried. But she does date sometimes. We never hear from my dad. All I know about him is that he's an artist. Well, sort of. He's probably a starving artist, and for all I know, he could be an alcoholic or maybe he's even into drugs. Who knows."

"So that's where you get your artistic talents?"

I shrug. "I don't know."

"Don't be so modest, Kara. You're really good. I think you're the best in the class."

"Really?" I feel slightly stunned by this high praise. "Hey, thanks. I never would've thought that of myself."

"Well, you're really good. And I'm sure it won't go to your head if I tell you."

Suddenly I'm feeling a little better about tonight and my life in general. And I'm actually wondering why someone like Edgar Peebles wouldn't make a perfectly acceptable best friend. I mean he's kind and thoughtful and sensitive. I think he must have a pretty strong feminine side, for a guy anyway. Although I don't really think he's gay. Really, he'd probably make a great best friend.

Just the same, I think I'd prefer a female best friend. Probably because that's what I'm comfortable with and I think life would just be simpler that way. Especially when it comes to sharing clothes or makeup or personal concerns that might be embarrassing to mention around the opposite sex. I suppose I really need a girl to hang with.

But then who am I to be so picky when I hardly have a friend to call my own anyway? Wouldn't having Edgar as a best friend be better than nothing? And he is kind of cute. So now I'm looking at this semi-geeky guy and thinking he might be just the ticket. And I wonder if he'd be interested, or how a person even brings something like this up. I mean do you just say, "Hey, wanna be best friends?" or what?

Then as we're paying the bill and getting ready to leave, I remember how Edgar said he *already* has a best friend. I think those were his exact words too. He said he didn't need a human best friend because he has *Jesus* for a best friend. It's a little hard to wrap my mind around this slippery concept. I don't actually think he's saying that he doesn't need anyone else in his life. But then when I think about it, Edgar has always seemed pretty self-sufficient. And I don't recall ever seeing him hanging with friends. Of course, I've always assumed that had more to do with his image.

As Edgar drives me home, I am considering this whole Jesus-as-best-friend concept. To be perfectly honest, it sounds just a little too good to be true. And you know what they say about that. Besides, how exactly does one go about becoming best friends with someone who's invisible and silent and fairly intimidating anyway? What good would it even do? I'm thinking I might as well talk to a wall or a lamppost. Really, I think I need a flesh-and-blood friend who I can laugh and cry with, someone who can listen and understand, someone who knows how to just hang together and have a good time without doing anything special. Now is that too much to ask?

twenty

THE IDEA OF HAVING ANOTHER WHOLE, LONG, LONELY WEEKEND LOOMing before me is fairly daunting as I lie in bed on this dreary Saturday morning. It's like I'm afraid to even get up. Like I don't even want to begin this day that promises to be so boring and empty. Did I mention that it's raining outside?

And I already know that Mom has a sales seminar to go to. She's probably already left by now. And Bree plans to hang with Sunny again today. Nice that someone has friends.

I entertain myself by thinking of things I might possibly do today.

1. I could clean my room. Not.
2. I could redecorate my room. Doubtful.
3. I could go to the library and do homework. Ugh.
4. I could take a soggy run. Yuck.
5. I could surprise Mom by cleaning house. *Puh-leeze.*
6. I could get on a bus and see where it takes me. Interesting . . .

But the phone is ringing now, and since it sounds like Bree is in the shower, I suppose it's up to me to answer. And who knows, maybe it's someone wanting to be interviewed for the position of Kara's new best friend.

"Hi, Kara?"

"Yeah."

"This is Suzy next door. I know this is last-minute, but something unexpected just came up. Could you possibly babysit the boys all day today?"

And so it's settled. I guess it's better than nothing and at least I'll make some money. But honestly, what a pitiful excuse for a life.

Fortunately Jeffy and Justin seem happy to see me and the day goes fairly well, although Suzy's apartment is pretty much trashed by five o'clock. I'm actually sort of relieved when she calls and asks if I could feed the boys dinner and put them to bed since she's afraid she'll be gone later than expected.

Suzy doesn't get home until nearly midnight. And by then I have her apartment looking even better than when she left. I've discovered this is a good way to get paid extra when babysitting. And it works because Suzy is quite grateful and generous when she gets home.

"Thanks so much, Kara. You're the best babysitter in the world."

I smile and say goodnight and wonder if that's the kind of thing I'd like to be remembered for—"the best babysitter in the world." Hmmm.

Somehow I make it through the next day and then I wonder why I dreaded the weekend so much when I realize I now have a whole week of school to face. And really, which is worse? A couple of days without friends or an entire week? Besides that, I remember how angry Betsy Mosler was and how she probably really hates my guts now.

As I walk to school, I replay the unhappy events at the dance. I replay the things that Jordan said to me, and by the time I reach the school I am ready to turn around and go home.

But what has really changed? I mean, Jordan was ignoring me before and she'll probably ignore me even more now. So what? Still, as hard as I try to make myself believe that I am nonchalant, that I don't care, that those stupid, shallow kids have absolutely no hold over me, I know that it's not true. Because I do care. I do worry and fret over the snide little comments and the hurtful looks. I do wish that everyone could just be nice to everyone for a change. And here's what's really pathetic: I still wish that life would return to what it was last summer. I still wish that Jordan and I were best friends. Why am I such a fool?

I'm early enough for English that I can slip into the back of the room, open my book, and pretend to be absorbed by *Ivanhoe*. I glance up through the strand of hair that's fallen across my face to observe Jordan and a couple of her friends walking into class. As usual they are laughing and joking. It seems their life is nothing but one big, happy party. And it makes me sick. They chat with Mr. Parker, acting like they really love his fish tie, but I'm sure it's just a big schmoozing act for the benefit of their midterm grades. I'm sure they really think he looks ridiculous in a tie that resembles a dead fish.

I watch them as they take seats, all clustered together as if they might feel isolated or alone should they have to sit a desk or two apart from each other. Poor things. I feel so sorry for them.

I notice that I'm chewing on my pencil again. It looks like it's been through the shredder. It's a recently acquired habit that I'm not terribly thrilled about but seem unable to shake. I'm sure it's stress-related, and once again I can feel the tightness in my stomach and my head is beginning to throb. I realize that I need to get the upper hand in this thing. I can't let this consume me. But how do I not?

When first period ends, I wait until Jordan and her friends have exited before I make my way to the door. But just as I'm coming out the door I see the girls clustered together again. I can tell by the way their heads are tilted toward each other that they are gossiping. I'd never really considered Jordan to be into gossip. I suppose it's because we never had much to gossip about, but at the time I probably assumed it was because we were above such petty and juvenile behavior. Seems I've been wrong about a lot of things.

I see no alternative than to walk directly past them and so I do. But as I do, I see them pause and I notice Jordan looking my way. But it's the expression that totally devastates me. It's like she's looking right through me. Like I don't even exist, or maybe she wishes that she'd never known me, never been my friend, or that I was simply dead. They say that words are painful, but I think looks can kill.

As I walk toward economics class, I feel that I am dying a slow and painful death. It's like the life is draining out of me and I don't even care. I know I'm probably just being melodramatic, but I am so convinced that my life totally sucks that I wonder why I don't just turn around and walk out of here and go lie down on some train tracks somewhere. Unfortunately we don't have any train tracks nearby.

Somehow I make it to art class. But I can still feel that look from Jordan, still burning through me, cutting me to the core. I pull out my latest art project and begin to work. I don't even bother to go join the others at the big table in back. I don't really want to talk to anyone today. And I'm thinking I'll just duck out of here when class is over and skip the lunch-bunch thing. Maybe I'll just go home and go to bed. Maybe I'll sleep until I'm eighteen then get up and see if I can get accepted into a decent college. Or join the army. I think I might make a good soldier.

"What's up?" asks Edgar. He's leaning onto the table and looking at my sketch.

I just shrug without looking at him.

"You okay, Kara?"

I can hear the concern in his voice, but somehow that's just *not* what I need right now. In fact, I'm sure it's going to make me cry if he keeps this up.

"I just want to work," I manage to say in a husky voice that probably sounds as if I've been out smoking in the parking lot with Amy's friends.

"Okay." He backs off now and I think my act must be quite convincing.

But now I am unable to sketch. All I can do is look at my half-finished project and the glossy photo that I was attempting to recreate. And before long both of these images become blurry. Then I go up to Ms. Clark and ask permission to go to the bathroom. But instead of going to the bathroom, I just walk out the side door, across the school grounds, through the security gates, and toward home. I unlock the apartment, go directly to my room, and climb into bed. I feel like my body is made of heavy stones and I am so very, very tired. I hope that I can sleep all day. Maybe all week. Maybe forever.

twenty-one

I'M AWAKENED BY THE PHONE RINGING. IT'S LIGHT OUTSIDE AND I WONDER what day it is as I stumble through the apartment to answer the stupid phone and silence its obnoxious ringing.

"Kara?" It's a guy's voice.

"Yeah."

"This is Edgar. I hope I'm not disturbing you."

"I was asleep."

"Sorry. I was kind of worried about you today. I noticed that you left art early and then I didn't see you around anywhere after that. Are you okay?"

"Okay?" I consider this word and wonder what it really means.

"Are you sick?" he persists.

"Not exactly. Maybe."

"Are you depressed?"

Bingo, I'm thinking. *You got that right.* But instead I just say, "I don't know."

"Well, I've really been praying for you, Kara. I feel like God is really trying to get your attention. And as hard as things might feel to you, I think it's all going to work together for something really great."

"Something really great?" I'm sure he can hear the disbelief in my voice. But I don't care.

"Yeah. I think you're going to invite Jesus to be your best friend too. And then your life is going to really improve."

I want to laugh at this, and I even make a feeble attempt which unfortunately sounds more like I'm gasping or gagging or strangling.

"You okay?"

"Yeah, Edgar, I'm fine."

"Anyway, I wanted to invite you to a Bible study tonight. It's at my church—"

"Oh, I don't know about—"

"It's with high school and college kids and it's really pretty cool, Kara. Wouldn't you please just give it a try? Just this once? And if you don't like it, I'll never ask you to come again."

"Meaning that you plan to keep asking me until I give it a try."

"Something like that."

"And it'll get you off my back if I come tonight?"

"Yeah."

I consider this and for whatever reason I finally agree to go. I think it's mostly to shut him up. I mean, I like having Edgar for my friend, but I just wish he'd put a lid on the religious stuff.

"Great. I'll pick you up a little before seven."

So it's all settled. I am going with Edgar Peebles, class nerd, to a Bible study at a church. Just when I thought Kara Hendricks had sunk about as low as she could get. Go figure.

It's not until I'm sitting next to Edgar on this long, lumpy blue sofa that I realize I never bothered to brush my hair, let alone my teeth. Not that I cared earlier, since it's only a Bible study for heaven's sake! But then when I get here and see all these kids who look fairly normal and almost cool, I begin to feel a bit self-conscious at my lack of personal hygiene, not to mention fashion sense. Now that's pretty weird.

So I sit here pretending that I'm just another lump in the sofa as I listen to this guy named Mike speaking. And to my surprise some of the things he's saying make sense. It's like he's talking to me, like he knows how I'm feeling inside.

"You see, God designed us to feel lonely," Mike's saying. "And it seems like a bad thing at first, but it's really not. God created this space, this vacuum, inside of us that will always feel empty and void and aching. So naturally we try to fill this space up. We might try to fill it with activities or even material things. But usually we try to fill it with friends or romantic relationships. But whatever we fill it with will eventually let us down. Then we become lonelier than ever."

I glance over at Edgar now, wondering if he told Mike about me so that he could preach a sermon targeted at the new girl. But Edgar looks oblivious as he listens intently, as if Mike is directing this little sermon to him. Then Mike begins telling us about a time in high school when he thought he was in love with this girl. They went together for three years then she broke up and broke his heart.

"I thought I was going to die," he says, and I can hear him choking up a bit. "It's still hard to talk about, but I think I need to share this." He pauses to take a sip of coffee now. "You see, I had tried to fill that void inside of me with Sarah. And I suppose it put a lot of pressure on our relationship. It's like I was looking to her for everything. I thought all my fulfillment in life was supposed to come from her. I guess it's no wonder that she broke up with me." He smiles now and I wonder why any girl in her right mind would break up with this great-looking guy.

"Anyway," he continues. "I was totally crushed when she broke up. I didn't want to do anything or see anyone. I guess I was pretty depressed, but it eventually turned me back to God. And it wasn't long before I realized that I had been trying to put Sarah in the place that is designed for only God to fill. When I invited Jesus into my heart, I realized that he was the one I needed to go to for my fulfillment. He is the only one who can make that space inside of me whole. For the first time in my life I understood that God made a special space inside of me for Jesus to fill. And now Jesus really is my best friend."

I glance over at Edgar again and this time he is smiling and nodding. I can tell that he totally relates. It's what he was basically telling me the other day. Only I suppose it makes more sense now.

Mike continues talking about how he knows God is going to bring the perfect girl into his life someday, but that it will be different. He won't be expecting her to be his everything anymore. "She'll have to be in second place to Jesus," he continues. "But that second place is actually a higher position than where I'd put Sarah, because it's the right position. It's like everything is in order, in its proper place." He glances around the room now, making eye contact with each kid there.

Well, except for me, because I quickly look down when he comes to the lumpy blue sofa. I'm afraid he's going to ask us something individually, like he's looking for some kind of a personal response here, which I am frankly not into. I do *not* wish to be subjected to coercion or to become a public spectacle. I think I would walk out if that happened.

But fortunately this doesn't seem to be his plan. "I know that you guys can relate to this. Because I know that you realize you are made this same way. Now some of you have already filled this empty void with God and you are living happier and more fulfilled lives. Oh, I know that it's not all perfect, but it's a whole lot better than before. Right?" And most of the kids say "right" or "amen."

Then Mike continues. "But some of you are still struggling with that lonely emptiness. You are still trying to fill that space, maybe it's with a boyfriend or a girlfriend, or whatever you think it will take to make your life happy. And like I said, there's nothing wrong with those things. In their proper places. But they will never fit or fill the space that God designed for Jesus to live in. Until you invite Jesus into your heart, you will always be striving for something else. Something or someone newer, better, nicer. But, believe me, you'll never find it. Not until you find Jesus."

Now Mike is opening a big, black leather Bible. "I'm going to read you something from the book of Revelation. This is an open invitation that Jesus offers to all of us. It's in chapter three, verse twenty. Listen. 'Behold, I stand at the door and knock. If anyone hears My voice and opens the door, I will come in to him and dine with him, and he with Me.'"

Mike pauses now, looking around the room again. This time I don't look down. I am too interested in what he's going to say next. "This invitation that Jesus offers might sound strange to you at first. I mean, here he is, saying that he wants to come inside of you and to eat and drink. You might be thinking, what's up with that? But think about it for a minute. Isn't that what friends do together? I mean, if you're really comfortable with each other it's no big deal to grab a burger together or share a pizza. In fact, it's a fun way to spend time with someone you like. Think about it: Would you enjoy sharing a meal with someone you can't stand? So, what Jesus is saying is, hey, I want to be your friend. I want to be part of your life. I'm knocking on your door. Why don't you let me come in?"

Now, to my total surprise, I can feel tears streaming down my cheeks. I look down at my lap and take in a deep breath. What's going on here?

"Let's pray," Mike is saying now. "Dear Jesus, thank you for loving us so much that you want to be an intimate part of our lives. Thank you that you enjoy our company so much that you want to spend lots and lots of time with us. Thank you for wanting to become our best friend. Thank you for laying down your life just so that you could be part of ours. Amen."

Fortunately, I have a chance to dry my tears while Mike is praying. Still, I think something is going on inside of me. I don't know how to describe it, but I have this sense that maybe Jesus really is knocking on my heart. And I don't think it's a coincidence that I came here tonight. But I'm just not sure what to do next. Where do I go from here?

Kids are moving around now. Some are helping themselves to more donuts and coffee and apple cider. But I'm just standing by the door, part of me wishing that Edgar was ready to leave and part of me wanting to do something. I'm just not sure what.

"This is Kara," says Edgar to Mike now.

"Hi, Kara," says Mike. "Mike Greyson. Glad you could join us. So what do you think of our little Bible study group?"

"I'm not sure," I say. "It's all kind of new to me."

He nods. "That's cool. Do you have any questions about anything you heard tonight?"

I consider this. "Well, sort of."

He smiles. "Go ahead, shoot away. I can even handle criticism if that's where you're going."

"No, that's not it. I guess I'm just wondering, I mean if all that you said is true, then how do you go about this thing? How do you open the door and let Jesus come inside. I mean, like, where's the doorknob?"

This makes Mike laugh. But not in a mean way. "That is a great question. Where's the doorknob?" He scratches his head now as if he's really trying to figure this out. "First of all, I'd say it's on the inside. And the nature of a doorknob is that you have to grab onto it and turn it to make it open. It's not going to open by itself, is it?"

I shake my head, although I'm not totally sure I'm following him here.

"So you have to make a choice, Kara. You have to decide whether or not you want to actually reach for that doorknob and open the door. If you really want to open the door, then you simply make that choice. And then you invite Jesus to come inside of you. And once you've done that, your life will never be the same again. Right, Edgar?"

Edgar nods now. "Yeah, that's what happened with me."

"Me too," says a girl named Chelsea that I vaguely know from school. "I've been a Christian for about a year now and it just keeps getting better and better."

"You guys make it sound so easy," I say with uncertainty. "Don't you ever have doubts about any of this?"

"Of course," says Mike. "Faith is like this journey you're taking. It has its ups and downs. You get attacked by doubt sometimes. But each time you face it and continue moving forward, you just get stronger."

Several others join in now, telling of various doubts and struggles they've experienced and how they eventually conquered them. All in all, it's quite a convincing act. Not that I think it's an act exactly. Actually I think these kids are sincere. I even think that what they're saying is probably true. And it's obviously the right thing for them. But does that really mean it's the right thing for me?

I stew over all these things as Edgar drives me home in his uncle's old black Caddie again. The rain is pouring down in sheets now and the windshield wipers are swiping back and forth at an amazing speed.

"Thanks for coming with me tonight," he says when we reach the apartment complex. "I hope you're not feeling confused by all this."

I shrug. "I'm not sure what I'm feeling, Edgar."

He smiles. "Well, I'll be praying for you."

I don't know whether to thank him or not. But I say goodnight and dash through the pouring rain toward the apartment.

Fortunately, Mom and Bree are glued to the TV, watching some new reality show that looks pretty stupid if you ask me. I tell them goodnight and head straight for my room. I peel off my soggy sweatshirt and kick off my wet shoes then sit down on my bed and try to figure out exactly what I'm feeling right now.

I take a deep breath and slowly exhale. I do this several times, hoping to clear my thoughts and calm my head. For some reason, tonight has stirred up all sorts of emotions in me. And I'm just not sure whether it's a good thing or not. As I sit, I begin to realize that there is one predominate feeling that keeps rising to the surface. It is a longing.

Longing.

It's not a word I normally use. But I know that it's the right one. I *am* longing for something. Or rather someone. I am longing for someone to accept me and love me and to be my best friend. I guess I've known this all along. But for some reason it seems even more urgent tonight.

I think that I am longing for Jesus. But even as these thoughts pass through my mind, I am questioning it. How can this be? I don't know anything about Jesus. Why would I suddenly long for him to come inside of me? Have I been brainwashed?

I take in a few more deep breaths and attempt once more to calm myself. But the longing remains. It is not going away.

"I stand at the door and knock . . . " To my surprise, I remember those words, and I suddenly envision Jesus standing out in the pouring rain just patiently knocking on my door. I know how it feels to be standing on the outside, just wishing someone would open the door and let you in. I know about the frustration of waiting and hoping that your friend will change her mind and open the door and say, "Hey, come on in! What have you been waiting for?" I know the disappointment when it doesn't happen.

And suddenly I know that I don't want to do that to Jesus. And I don't want him to do it to me. So I imagine myself reaching for that doorknob and giving it a twist as I pull open the door.

Then to my surprise, I actually say, out loud, "Come on in, Jesus." I take in a quick breath. "Come inside and make yourself at home."

Then I sit and wait and soon I am crying again, but these seem to be happy tears. And a warm feeling begins to flow through me, almost like a gentle rush of electrical current and I realize that I've done it. I've really done it! I've invited Jesus into my heart. And he is really here.

I'm not sure if anyone else would call it praying, but I think that's what I'm doing now. I am thanking Jesus for loving me and coming to live inside of me. And before long I am telling him about how lonely I've been and how hurt I've been and by the time I go to bed, I feel so much better.

It's almost scary feeling this good. Because I'm afraid it won't last. I'm afraid that when I get up tomorrow morning I'll feel just as bummed as I felt this afternoon. I'm scared to death that it will all just fade away and I'll be the same old lonely Kara Hendricks that I was before. And quite honestly, I just don't know if I can handle it.

twenty-two

To my complete surprise, I woke up quite early this morning and I actually felt happy. It's kind of weird too, since I really haven't felt happy in weeks. And I don't think it's my birthday or anything special. It takes me a minute or two before I realize what's going on. Then I remember how I invited Jesus into my heart last night, right here in my own bedroom.

Then I feel this cool rush of excitement. And not only do I feel happy, but I feel unexpectedly energetic too. So, I pull on my sweats and lace up my running shoes and I zip outside for a quick run. The sky is gray and there are puddles everywhere, but I feel elated as I leap and jump over them. It almost feels like I can fly!

When I get back to the apartment I still have time to get the first shower before Mom and Bree are even out of bed. It's amazing.

"What's up with you?" asks Bree as she spies me humming in the kitchen while I pour myself a tall glass of orange juice.

"Just feeling good," I say with a smile. I have no doubts that I am totally confusing my little sister with my erratic behavior, but that's okay. She might figure it out in time. Maybe I'll even figure out how to tell her soon.

When my mom comes into the kitchen I realize that I need to tell her about skipping school yesterday. I'm not terribly proud of what I did, but considering the circumstances and how I felt at the time, I think it should be understandable.

"I was just really depressed, Mom," I finish up my explanation. "But, honestly, I don't think it'll happen again."

She's looking at me curiously now. "And you're feeling better today?"

"Yeah, I feel great today."

"And you're not taking drugs or anything?"

I know she's only partially joking. "No, Mom, this is a natural high." Okay, maybe it's really a supernatural high. The truth is, I'm not really sure how to classify these things.

"Well, I know you've been feeling pretty down lately, Kara. And it is nice to see you feeling better. Maybe you just needed a mental health day yesterday. I have to take those from my work too, you know. Okay, I'll write you an excuse if you're positive that you won't play hooky again."

"I really don't think I will," I assure her. Now part of me wants to tell her why, but I guess I still have this tiny reservation that I might be imagining the whole thing about Jesus being inside of me. And so I've decided to let some time go by before I go announcing to the world that I have "become a Christian." But I do think I might tell Edgar. And maybe even Felicia too. Or not. We'll see. Anyway, I am totally excited about today and ready to go to school. *Let my life begin!*

Today as I walk down the hall I hold my head up high. I don't care who I see or what they may or may not be thinking about me. All I care about is the fact that Jesus is inside me. I really believe that he is.

I see Jordan walking toward me now. Ashley and Shawna are with her. Normally this is just the type of scenario that would send ice water running through my veins. But today I am totally calm.

"Hey, Jordan," I say to her as I smile and wave. "Hey, Ashley and Shawna."

I get a thrill to see the slightly stunned looks on their faces. And I'm not terribly surprised to see that Shawna and Ashley don't answer. But at least Jordan says, "Hey," back. Of course, I'm sure those girls never expected the mealy-mouthed Kara Hendricks to actually speak to them first, and in public too. But why not?

I take a front-row seat in English and actually pay attention as Mr. Parker lectures in his usual monotone voice. I even take notes. It's occurring to me that my midterm grades have suffered this fall and I plan to make up for it now.

The morning progresses in much this same way. And here's what's really weird. I'm actually beginning to think that people are way friendlier today. I've seen a lot more smiles and heard more greetings than ever before. I don't even remember kids being this nice when I was best friends with Jordan, and she was pretty friendly with everyone. I wonder what has changed. Or is it just me?

By the time art rolls around I feel as if I'm about to burst. I can't wait to tell Edgar the news. I know he will be happy for me. But to my dismay, he is not here.

"That's odd," says Felicia when she notices he's missing. "I don't think Edgar has ever been absent."

"I hope he's okay," I say. But I'm sure he must be. After all, he is Edgar.

I work on my sketch and stay and have lunch with Felicia and Amy. It's sort of nice just hanging with the girls today, although I do miss Edgar. And Amy seems a little down and Felicia is really absorbed in her painting of a rose.

I consider telling them about inviting Jesus into my heart, but for some reason it feels important to share this news with Edgar first. And so I stay quiet. But in my quietness I have discovered that I am having this ongoing conversation with Jesus. And it is so cool. It feels like he's interested in everything about me. It feels like he's really becoming my best friend. And it keeps making me smile.

"What are you so happy about today, Kara?" asks Amy as lunchtime is about to end. "You in love or something?"

"In love with life," I tell her.

She peers at me with interest. "You on something?"

I shake my head. "Just a natural high."

She rolls her eyes at me now. "Yeah, yeah, sure. You're probably just going bipolar on us. I have this cousin who's manic-depressive and she can be just flipping crazy sometimes."

"Well, that's not what's going on with me," I assure her. "But thanks anyway."

Then the bell rings and I clean up my stuff and head on my way. I see Jordan again, alone this time, and I actually pause to ask her how she's doing.

Looking at me funny, as if she thinks I might be a card or two short of a full deck, she answers, "I'm okay. But what's with you?"

"Just feeling happy is all," I say with a smile. Then I turn and walk away. And for the first time since Jordan and I quit being friends I feel absolutely no regrets. It's not that I hate her or anything, but I just don't feel like I so desperately need her anymore. For the first time since kindergarten I feel like I am a whole and complete person. Or nearly. But I realize this is only because I've allowed Jesus to come inside of me and fill up that old empty hole.

The second half of my day goes just as well as the first and I am now wondering why I didn't invite Jesus into my heart years ago. Think of all the pain and suffering I might have avoided. Oh, well, at least it's done now. And I can look forward to having this for the rest of my lifetime.

I still wonder about Edgar though. I haven't seen him anywhere at school today. I wish I had his phone number, and I wonder if Amy might. Then I remember that she did his makeover last week. Perhaps she even knows where he lives. I search for her in the halls after school is out but can't find her anywhere.

Finally, I remember her favorite haunt out by the parking lot. And sure enough, there she is with several of her friends, all enjoying their after-school cigarette. Although as I get closer I notice that Amy's the only one not lighting up.

"Hi, Amy," I call out as I approach. I can feel their curious stares and I know they're wondering who I think I am to come onto their turf. But I just wave and smile as if I'm welcome here. And to my surprise they lighten up.

"Sorry to interrupt," I tell Amy. "But I wondered if you know Edgar's phone number."

"You're gonna call Edgar Peebles?" says a guy wearing a black ski hat pulled low down on his forehead.

"Yeah." I look him in the eye as I answer. "Edgar's my friend and I'm a little worried about him."

The ski-hat dude snickers but doesn't say anything else.

"I don't have his phone number," says Amy. "But I know where he lives."

"Can you give me his address?" I reach into my backpack for a pen.

"I can do better than that." Then Amy elbows Ski-hat Dude. "Max, can you give me a lift?"

He nods. "You wanna go now?"

Amy looks at me. "You in?"

"Sure."

The next thing I know I'm climbing into the backseat of an old Toyota Corolla that smells like dirty socks and cigarettes.

"Wanna licorice?" offers Amy as she holds out a package of red licorice.

"Thanks."

She grins as she chomps down on one. "This is my latest stop-smoking attempt. But at the rate I'm going, I'll probably put on thirty pounds before I'm totally smoke-free."

"That's cool that you're quitting," I tell her as I look around for the seatbelt. I'm not sure what I think about Max's driving, but as he swerves around the corner I'm not too embarrassed to dig around until I locate and fasten my seatbelt.

Edgar's house is on the other side of town. It's a rundown neighborhood where small houses are packed together between narrow, weedy yards. And their siding looks like cardboard.

"That's it," says Amy as she jabs Max in the shoulder. "The green one on the right."

"You want me to stick around for you?" he asks as he pulls out a package of Camels.

"Sure," says Amy. "Edgar might not even be home."

So the two of us walk up the narrow cement path to Edgar's door and Amy knocks, quite loudly. The house doesn't look too big and I'm sure whoever lives here could hear her knocking clear into the back. We think we can hear someone moving around in there, and after a couple of minutes the door opens, and there is Edgar wearing a torn pair of gray sweat pants. That's all. No shirt, no shoes, no smile.

"Hi, Edgar," I say in a meek voice. "Are you okay? We missed you at school and were worried . . . "

"What's up, Edgar?" Amy takes her typical no-nonsense approach. "You don't look so hot."

He shrugs and I notice that his eyes are red. I think he's actually been crying. "Edgar," I say, reaching out for his hand. "What's wrong?"

His face crumbles now and he turns and goes back into the house, leaving the front door open, I assume, as an invitation. So I walk in and Amy follows.

It's dim and gloomy in the living room. The dingy-looking drapes are drawn and no lights are on. It takes a moment for my eyes to adjust to the semi-darkness. Then I notice Edgar sitting hunched on an old red sofa that dips down in the middle. His head is bent forward and his hands hang limply between his knees. He looks totally destitute, like he's just lost his best friend. But somehow I can't believe that could be true. I just don't think that Jesus could've abandoned Edgar like this.

I sit down on the sofa next to Edgar and Amy sits on the opposite side. The three of us sit there for a few minutes in silence. I can tell by the movement in his shoulders that Edgar is crying, although he barely makes a sound. But it's just breaking my heart to see him like this. Finally I can't stand it a moment longer. I turn and look at him.

"Edgar," I plead, "please, tell us what's wrong. Is there something we can do to help?"

But he simply shakes his head. "There's nothing you can do, Kara. Nothing anyone can do now."

"What about Jesus?" I demand and he looks at me with surprise. "Huh?"

"I know that he's your best friend, Edgar," I continue. "Surely there's something that Jesus can do to help you."

"It's too late," is all he says.

"Too late for what?" asks Amy. "Tell us what's going on here, Edgar."

He takes in a deep breath now, holds it then slowly exhales. "Too late for my mom," he finally says.

"What happened?" I ask. "Is she still in prison?" I notice Amy's eyes flash curiosity and I toss her a glance that says "later." Hopefully Edgar doesn't mind that I let this slip out.

"What's going on with your mom?" I ask again, more gently this time. And I place my hand on his shoulder. "Come on, Edgar, we're your friends. You can talk to us."

He looks at me now as if he's gauging my words, as if he's weighing in on my authenticity.

"Really," I reassure him. "And if it helps anything, I wanted you to know that I did it, Edgar. Last night, after I got home, I did it. I invited Jesus into my heart. I wanted you to be the first one I told. Only I was hoping it would be a happier occasion."

He nods. "That's cool, Kara. I'm really happy for you." Then he puts his head down and begins to sob again.

I rub his back and just wait. But as I wait I am silently talking to Jesus, just like I've been doing on and off all day. I am asking Jesus to help me be a better friend to Edgar. And I'm asking him to help Edgar get through whatever it is that's making him so upset.

Finally Edgar stops crying and looks up, just staring blankly across the shabby little living room. He wipes his hands on his cheeks then slowly shakes his head. "My mom was up for parole yesterday. It was denied. But I guess she didn't take the news so well" — his voice breaks — "and she . . . she hung herself last night. She's dead."

Amy lets loose with a four-letter word.

"Oh, Edgar," I say, reaching for his hand. "Oh, I'm so sorry." Now I am crying too. Just silently sitting there and holding his hand and crying. I'm not sure how long we sit there like that, but I notice that Amy is sobbing too. So I put my arms around both of them and now we are all huddled together in a big group hug, just the three of us crying together. I don't know what else to do.

After a while, how long I don't know, we stop crying and one-by-one lean back into the sofa.

"Thanks," says Edgar with a sigh. "Thanks for coming, you guys. I don't know when I've ever needed someone as much as today. I mean, Kara is right, I do have Jesus and I know that he's here with me and that he'll help me through this. But it makes a difference having real, physical people in your life too. Thanks."

"Is there anything we can do?" I ask.

"Not that I know of. My dad kind of flipped out last night. He took off around midnight and I'm pretty sure he's fallen off the wagon by now. I think he's blaming himself for everything. It's a real mess."

"I'm so sorry," I say again.

"Man," says Amy as if she's still taking it all in. "Your life really sucks, Edgar."

"Yeah, I guess it looks like that."

"When did you last eat?" I ask suddenly. I'm not even sure why. Maybe it was just seeing his ribs on his back, like I was thinking he was malnourished.

He shrugs. "Yesterday. Last night, I guess."

"Well, why don't you get on some clothes and we'll take you out for some food. It won't do anyone any good if you starve to death."

"Good idea, Kara," agrees Amy. She stands and pulls Edgar to his feet. "Besides, Max is probably getting impatient."

Before long, we're all parked around a sticky table at

McDonald's. Even Max joins us and seems honestly concerned about Edgar's problems.

"My Uncle Rick wants me to come live with him," says Edgar. "But I'll only do that if my dad's really fallen off the wagon for good. I'm thinking last night might just be a one-time thing. You can't really blame him, you know."

Amy pats Edgar's hand. "No, you can't. I've used all kinds of lame excuses to get drunk. But something like this could really rock your world."

"I've had lots of excuses for getting wasted," agrees Max. "But nothing as big as what's happened to you and your dad. Man, it's such a shame."

We spend about an hour at McDonald's and it seems like Edgar is beginning to feel a little better.

"I think I should get back now," he says. "In case my dad comes home, you know. But thanks for the food, you guys."

So we drive him back home and Amy and I both hug him again and tell him we love him.

"And I'll be praying for you and your dad," I promise.

"And if I knew how to pray or who to pray to, I would too," says Amy. "As it is I'll be thinking good thoughts about you."

"Thanks," says Edgar.

"And you've got our phone numbers now, so you call us if you need anything," I remind him. "You know that we're here for you. We're your friends, Edgar."

He nods. "I can really see that. Thanks."

And then we leave. The car is quiet and somber as Max drives toward my apartment complex.

"Thanks for the ride, Max," I finally tell him. "I really appreci-ate it."

He smiles now. "No problem. See ya, Kara."

"Take care, Kara," says Amy.

I feel exhausted as I go up the steps to our apartment. And I feel sad. In some ways, it's not all that different from how I've felt in the past. Except that it's totally different too. It's like my exhaustion is coming from this deep place, a place where I have used all my energy and resources to do something that's really worthwhile. And my sadness, for a change, is not centered on myself and my problems. It's about Edgar and his mother and father.

It's almost five o'clock, but the apartment is quiet and it looks like no one else is home yet. So I go straight to my room and fall down on my bed and I pray and pray for Edgar and his dad. I pray for them until I fall asleep. But when I wake up I feel oddly refreshed and almost hopeful. This amazes me in light of what's happened to Edgar today. I'm thinking it can only be because of Jesus.

twenty-three

EDGAR'S DAD FINALLY CAME HOME. TO EVERYONE'S RELIEF HE HADN'T fallen off the wagon but had simply driven to the place where he and Edgar's mother had first met back in the eighties. Edgar thinks it was his dad's way of grieving, and shows that he actually loved his wife despite her drug problems.

The funeral for Edgar's mother is today, and Amy and Max and I have decided to go. My mom even wrote me an excuse to leave school early. Max and Amy said they're just ditching and will take the consequences, as usual. But I think it's cool that we will be there to show our support for Edgar, to remind him that he has friends. Edgar asked us not to mention his mom's suicide to anyone else at school and we're respecting his wishes. I felt a little bad for not telling Felicia, because I think she really cares about Edgar. But I can understand him not wanting everyone to know. I mean, what good would it do? And I'm sure Edgar doesn't want anyone's pity. Besides, it seems like a tragedy like this is talked about and taken really seriously at first, but then time passes and some less-than-thoughtful kids can get kind of calloused and mean. I sure don't want anyone saying anything cruel to Edgar.

After lunch Max drives us over to Edgar's church. After a lot of discussion, Edgar's dad finally agreed to have her funeral there. I guess it's Edgar's one concession in this whole sad affair. I have been praying all week that Jesus will help Edgar and his dad through this difficult time. I'm praying harder than ever today. I can't imagine how sad this funeral will be. I've only been to one funeral before and it was for Grandma Elena a few years ago. Of course, it was really sad too, but at least she was older and had died of "natural causes." Edgar's mom was only thirty-six (twelve years younger than my mom!) and she'd spent the last five years of her life in prison. So tragic.

The church is fairly empty when we get there, and so we sit close to the front. Out of respect for Edgar and his family I am wearing a black dress that I borrowed from my mom. I rarely wear dresses, but this occasion seemed to call for it. I noticed that Amy has toned down her usual dramatic appearance. She has on black jeans and a sweater and actually looks quite respectable for Amy. Max has on jeans and a leather jacket. All in all, I don't think we should be an embarrassment to Edgar.

Edgar already told me that the youth pastor, Mike, would be in charge of the service. I'm sure he'll do a good job. I look toward the front of the church now and notice that there is a dark wooden casket behind several bouquets of flowers. And in front stands an enlarged photograph of a very beautiful woman, which I'm sure must be Edgar's mother, but I am stunned by how pretty she is. Her smile is bright and vivacious and her auburn curls reach her shoulders, but the most striking feature is her large, dark eyes. I realize now that Edgar has his mother's eyes.

"Thank you all for coming today," says Mike as he adjusts the microphone. "This is a day of confusing emotions and before I say too much about Raven Marie Peebles, I would like to share a letter that's written by Raven's cellmate, Ms. Olivia Stockard." Mike clears his throat and reads.

"To Raven's Family and Friends:

"I'm sure that you, like me, are shocked and saddened by what Raven has done. But first I want to say how Raven was a good-hearted woman who never done no one, excepting herself, no harm. I knew her to be most kind and generous and a good listener too. I miss her already. And we might never understand why she done what she did, but, even so, I wanted to write down something to comfort you some in your time of distress.

"You see, like Raven, I made my share of mistakes in this life, and I be paying for them now. But I got my second chance when I was born again right here in this prison, and today I can say to you with blessed assurance that I be a new woman. A new creation. Now some of the gals here call me Preacher Girl and that be fine by me. And you can be sure that I have given Raven many a fiery sermon, and sometimes I think she even took it to heart. I also know that Edgar, her dear boy, wrote her many a fine letter telling her about the saving grace of our Lord Jesus.

"So, this morning as I sat here pondering over what will become of Raven now that she has taken life into her own hands, so to speak, it occurs to me that we human beings don't have all the answers. Only God knows what comes next. Raven had the good news preached at her over and over again. And who's to say it wasn't ringing in her ears during those last precious moments of her life. I know it's not for me to judge. And it's not for you neither. Anyway, I just wanted to share my thoughts with Raven's family. And I be praying for each of you. And for Raven too. Even though she's gone, I trust my precious Lord is smart enough to sort it all out when she shows up at his pearly gates. Sincerely, in Christ, Ms. Olivia Stockard."

Mike refolds the letter now. "No one could argue that Raven Peebles was a person who lived life on her own terms. She obviously made mistakes and suffered the consequences for them. But according to those who knew her best, she had a big heart and a kind spirit."

I listen as Mike tells more about Raven's unconventional past and how she grew up in a commune that had no electricity or telephones. He explains how she always considered herself a "free spirit" and how she thought that rules were meant to be broken.

"But based on this letter from Olivia, we can only hope and pray that Raven is all right now," continues Mike. "And we are instructed by the Lord Jesus Christ to not judge one another. Like Olivia said, we don't know what went through Raven's mind or heart in those last moments of her life. That is for God to do." Now Mike opens his Bible to a marked place. "This is what God's Word says about it in the book of John, verses sixteen and seventeen of chapter three: 'For God so loved the world that He gave His only begotten Son, that whoever believes in Him should not perish but have everlasting life. For God did not send His Son into the world to condemn the world, but that the world through Him might be saved.'"

Mike continues talking about God's mercy and forgiveness, and then we all bow our heads to pray. After that a couple from the church sing that Eric Clapton song about knowing someone's name in heaven and I'm sure that everyone is crying now. But it's a good kind of crying, I think. Then the couple sings a happier song that's also about heaven and the service comes to an end.

"Thanks for coming," says Edgar afterward.

I stare at him and feel certain that he looks several years older than the night we went to the dance. And maybe he is. "That was a nice letter from your mom's friend," I tell him.

He nods. "Yeah. It gives me hope. I mean I don't really know what she was thinking when she, well, you know. But there's this little part of me that hopes I'll see her again in heaven."

Amy and Max are both being unusually quiet right now, but it looks like Amy is fighting to hold back her tears.

"The church has some refreshments in the fellowship hall," says Edgar. "If you guys want to join us."

I can tell that Amy and Max aren't very comfortable here, but I'm relieved when they agree to come.

We hang around for almost an hour and Edgar introduces us to his dad, who seems very meek and quiet, as well as some of his church friends. And finally it's time to go. I think that Amy and Max are relieved to get out of the church, but I was actually starting to feel at home. In fact, I'm thinking that if Edgar doesn't mind, and I'm sure he won't, I'd like to try going to his church for a while.

It's cloudy and gray outside and just starting to sprinkle, but Max pauses in the parking lot to light up a Camel. He sucks in a deep breath then slowly exhales as if the smoke itself is going to revive his spirits.

"Don't you want one, Amy?" he asks, holding the pack out to her. "Or you still trying to quit?"

She looks longingly at the cigarette package and finally shakes her head. "Nah. I've gotten this far, I might as well see if I can do this."

"So, what did you think of the funeral?" Max says to no one in particular.

"It was kind of scary," says Amy in a serious tone.

"What do you mean?" I ask.

"It's hard to explain, but when I saw that picture of Raven—and, man, wasn't she gorgeous? I mean who would've thought that Edgar's mom would look like that?" She sadly shakes her head. "But anyway, when I saw that photo and then heard more about Raven's life and taking so many risks and the consequences she suffered and all that crud. Well, I guess it sort of hit home."

I nod without saying anything. But I think I understand.

"And I guess it kind of freaks me."

It's starting to rain harder now, and Max snuffs out his cigarette even though it's only half-smoked. "Let's go," he says in a gruff voice. I suspect he doesn't like where Amy's conversation seems to be heading.

Once she's in the front seat and the car is going, Amy turns around to look at me. "Do you really think Raven's in heaven, Kara?"

"I really don't know much about these things, but I actually do. And not just because of that letter from her friend, but I know what Edgar means, it's like I've got this feeling deep inside of me, like Raven's okay now, like maybe she's with God and finally at peace. You know?"

"Sort of, but I couldn't for the life of me explain why." Amy turns back around now. She slumps down into the passenger seat and Max continues to drive through the sheets of rain with only the sound of the windshield wipers filling the car.

Max drops me at home and I thank him for the ride and tell them both to have a good weekend. I wish I could think of something more encouraging to say to Amy. Especially since it seems like she's really bummed right now. But at least I can pray for her. That's more than I could do last week. And I remember how I had to go through my own tough times before I was ready to open the door to God. Maybe this struggle will help her to do the same.

I do plan to call Edgar tonight and tell him about what Amy said today. Somehow I think it will encourage him to know that she's thinking about these things too. And I know that he'll want to be praying for her. It would be so amazingly cool to think that something as sad and seemingly senseless as Edgar's mother's death could rock Amy's world hard enough to make her really wonder about God.

It's still raining outside, but I decide to go out and take a run anyway. I feel like I need to breathe some fresh air, and I think it'll help clear out my head. I return my mom's black dress to her closet then put on my sweats and lace up my shoes and just take off. I run my regular course for about twenty minutes then consider turning back toward home, but the rain is finally starting to let up, so I decide to hit the park for a cool-down.

As I jog toward the duck pond, I'm still thinking about the funeral and Edgar and his sad-looking dad. I'm also thinking about Max and Amy and even Raven. And I must admit that I'm feeling more and more bummed about everything. It doesn't quite make sense, because I do believe Jesus is still inside me, but it's like there's this wet blanket of sadness that's starting to cover me. It's almost suffocating and I don't know how to shake it off. I'm sure it's a result of the funeral today. I mean, who feels happy after a funeral? Just the same, I don't like it. It feels dark and lonely and hopeless.

Then I remember I can talk to my best friend about all this crud. And so I tell Jesus about my confused feelings. I tell him that I'm worried about my friends and I ask him to keep helping Edgar and his dad, as well as Amy and Max. I even go as far as to ask him if he can take away all the sadness in the world. But somehow I don't think that's going to happen. Still, I do feel better after this heart-to-heart chat. I feel like the weight is being lifted from me, like I can breathe again.

When I reach the duck pond, I notice that the clouds are finally starting to thin. And it's not long until the sun actually breaks through, creating a golden beam of light that makes me imagine a ladder that stretches up to heaven. Maybe it's the ladder that Raven has climbed. Or maybe it just swept her upward in one fantastic swoosh, faster than the speed of light.

I'm so caught up in my heavenly ladder theory that I almost don't notice the rainbow that's beginning to appear in the west. It's pale at first, but growing more vivid by the second. Bright pink and yellow and green and blue and purple. It's magnificent, the most glorious rainbow I've ever seen. I just stand by the duck pond and stare in amazed fascination. *Awesome, God!*

And somehow, I am absolutely certain that this is God's way of assuring all of us that Raven is perfectly safe with him now and that everything is okay for her. Anyway, that's what I believe. I sure hope that Edgar can see the rainbow. I know that they were planning to head out to the cemetery afterward. I hope and pray that they're standing there right now, witnessing this miraculous rainbow for themselves.

When I go home, I pull out an old set of colored pencils and attempt to re-create the beautiful scene I just saw at the park. Okay, it doesn't really look the same, and I probably got carried away with the rainbow colors, but I plan to give it to Edgar as a reminder that God is good. So incredibly good.

twenty-four

EDGAR IS BACK IN SCHOOL·ON MONDAY AND SEEMS TO BE HANDLING LIFE fairly well. Oh, I know he gets down sometimes, and he tells me that he still feels a little guilty for not going to visit his mother more while she was in prison.

"Man, when I think of all those years I wasted . . . " he says as we walk toward the art department together. "If I'd only known."

"But you were just a kid when she got sentenced, Edgar," I remind him. "That's a pretty heavy load, even for a grownup, but you can't blame yourself for what happened to her or even question what you did or didn't do before it was too late."

"I know," he says. "And I know that God's forgiven me. Still, I feel bad sometimes."

"Well, anytime you need to talk," I tell him as we enter the art room, "you know I'm here for you."

"Thanks, Kara." He almost smiles now. "And thanks for the picture. It's hanging in my bedroom."

By the end of the week, Edgar seems to be doing much better. He smiles more and seems to be back to trusting God for everything. Just like the old Edgar.

"I'm still not smoking," Amy announces during art on Friday. "It's been two weeks now and they say that if you can make it for two weeks, you can make it for life."

"Congratulations," says Felicia. "And your breath smells a lot better too."

"Thanks a lot," says Amy with a scowl.

It's Friday and I'm springing for pizza today. But I decide to walk outside with Edgar to wait for the delivery guy. It doesn't seem fair that he's stuck doing this all by himself all the time.

"Amy told me that she's been reading the Bible," he says after we're out in the hallway.

"Really?"

"Yeah. It was her own idea too. She said that if she's going to find out about God, it's going to be on her own terms."

"Kind of like what Mike said about your mom."

"Yeah. Amy really thinks that she and my mom are a lot alike."

"What do you think?"

He shrugs. "I don't know. I guess so. To be perfectly honest, I don't think I really knew my mom very well. I mean, I knew she was really intelligent, I could see that, but then it seemed like she was always doing something incredibly stupid too."

"Kind of like our Amy?"

He smiles now. "Yeah, I suppose so. Hey, isn't it cool that she quit smoking?"

"Yeah, now that really took some willpower."

"Not that God would treat her any differently or love her any less if she still smoked."

"Really?" I feel slightly confused now. "But doesn't God expect us to, well you know, live really good lives?"

"Of course," says Edgar as we reach the street.

We both sit down on the curb and watch for the little red van that brings the pizza.

Then Edgar continues, "I think God wants us to make good choices, Kara, and to take care of ourselves. But most of all I think he just wants us to love him and to let him into all the ordinary and sometimes gory details of our daily lives."

I nod as I point to the delivery van rattling down the street toward us. "Yeah. As you can probably guess, I don't know too much about all this God stuff yet, but I'll take your word for that, Edgar."

He laughs and waves to the pizza guy. "Hey, don't just take *my* word for it, Kara. Do like Amy's doing and read God's Word for yourself. Let him show you who he is and what he's all about."

And so the next morning, I call Edgar and ask him if he wants to go to the mall with me to help me pick out a Bible.

"I've never had one before," I confess with some embarrassment. I mean, it seems like if you're an American, you should probably have a Bible. But then my family's just never been like that. "And I really don't know anything about Bibles and I wouldn't want to, you know, get the wrong kind." I laugh nervously. "Is there a wrong kind?"

"I don't know about that, but I can show you the kind that Mike recommended to me."

"Cool." I sigh in relief. I'm so glad that Edgar is such an easygoing guy. I should've known he wouldn't make fun of my Bible ignorance. We agree to meet at the mall bus stop around noon. But I switch outfits several times before I leave the apartment. I mean, I realize this is definitely *not* a date or anything like that. Good grief, I'm the one who called Edgar. But for some reason how I look matters to me today.

I almost laugh at myself as I get on the bus. Now I ask you, who would've thought a couple of months ago that I, Kara Hendricks, would actually be concerned about my appearance when I was going to the mall to meet Edgar Peebles, of all people, so that I could pick out, and actually pay hard-earned babysitting money for, a Bible? Man, is life ever strange. But good. Very, very good.

We pick out what seems to me a nice Bible. It has what is called a study guide and all sorts of things to help me to understand what's going on better. I must admit it's a little overwhelming. Almost like learning a new language. But at the same time I'm excited. I'm thinking that knowledge about God must really be something.

"And don't worry," Edgar assures me as we get some lunch together. Thankfully we both agreed to skip the Sushi Bar. "You'll pick up a lot by going to church and youth group. Before long, you'll think you were raised on the Bible."

"How long have you been a Christian?" I ask.

"Only two and a half years," he says as he sticks his straw into his soda.

"Wow, you've learned a lot during that time."

We're chatting along happily when I notice Jordan and Betsy and Shawna standing at the edge of the food court. Now just a couple weeks ago, I would be feeling freaked by this, but today I just glance over and think nothing of it. In fact, I would even wave at them if they were a little bit closer. And I don't hate Jordan anymore. But more than that, I don't feel that horrible old obsession to gain back her friendship either. It's like I'm perfectly happy with the way my life is going without her. In fact, I've never been happier. Just the same, there is something about the way those three girls are standing, kind of erect and uneasy like, that makes me turn and look again.

Betsy and Shawna are facing Jordan, and the looks on both their faces are not friendly. I look at Jordan and realize she has that red-cheeked, wide-eyed look that she gets when she's about to start crying.

"What's wrong?" asks Edgar.

I nod in their direction. "Jordan and her friends. But it looks like something's wrong."

Edgar looks toward them. "Jordan seems upset."

Shawna's hands are on her hips now and it looks like she's confronting Jordan. In fact, it looks like she's actually yelling at her. Then Jordan just shakes her head and turns and walks away. I can tell by the way she's walking that she's extremely upset. Normally she has a very graceful, easy stride that she takes a certain amount of pride in, but she's flat-out clomping away from those two girls right now.

"I wonder what happened," I say to Edgar in a hushed voice, almost as if I think they're listening.

He shrugs. "You never know with *those* girls."

I look at him curiously, wondering how on earth he would know anything about *those* girls? "What exactly do you mean by that?"

He smiles now. "I know you probably think that geeks like me don't notice what's going on with the cool crowd, but for your information, we do. We just don't like to admit it."

"First of all, you're not a geek — "

He laughs. "Says who?"

"Says me."

He nods. "Okay. But I've probably had more time to observe the way kids treat each other than you have. And I suspect that Jordan has done something that's considered unacceptable within the code of the cool crowd."

"Like what?" I cannot imagine Jordan Ferguson ever doing anything that would be considered unacceptable by almost anyone. That is just not like Jordan.

"Hard to say. But it must be something pretty big for both those girls to turn on her at once. And chances are the whole group will be against her by Monday."

"No way." I shake my head. "I'll bet that it's all blown over by then. Jordan may have her faults when it comes to loyalty, but let me tell you, if she *wants* to be your friend, she can be an absolute diplomat at resolving differences. Wait and you'll see."

He raises his eyebrows. "Well, you know her better than I do."

So now I'm curious as to what will play out on Monday. But I suspect that Edgar is all wet when it comes to Jordan and her friends. I mean, really, how could someone like Edgar, a member of the chess club, have the slightest clue as to what goes on in the minds of girls like Jordan's cheerleading friends? I mean, really, it's even been pretty much a mystery to me.

twenty-five

EVERYONE IN SCHOOL — OKAY, EVERYONE WHO GIVES A RIP — SEEMS TO know that Jordan has been excommunicated from the *cool* crowd. However, I don't get the full scoop until art class, when Felicia finally fills me in.

"Jessie told me that Shawna Frye is fried," Felicia chuckles at her own lame humor, "because your old buddy Jordan has split up Shawna and Timothy Lawrence. And Shawna and Timothy have been going together since, like, eighth grade."

"I thought Jordan was going with Caleb Andrews," I say, revealing to everyone just how totally out of touch I really am.

"No," says Felicia with an air that's just slightly superior. "They broke up right after the Harvest Dance. Rumor is that Jordan was just using Caleb to get to Timothy. You know those two guys have been best friends for, like, forever."

"Best friends?" I consider the possibility of Jordan breaking up another old friendship then just shake my head. Go figure!

Edgar winks at me from across the table. "What did I tell you?"

"Too bad you didn't lay a wager," I tease him. "You could've cleaned up big time."

He grins. "Lucky for you I'm not a betting man."

"So what do you think will happen now?" I ask him.

He seems to consider this. "First of all, I think Jordan will make an effort to keep her position in the group. But that will be tough since she's the newcomer. I think the group will be divided, but the majority will be on Shawna's side since she's got more history with them. There'll probably be a lot of gossip and backbiting going on. How it ends is anybody's guess."

Felicia looks fairly surprised at his perceptive take on this whole thing. "Man, you're good, Edgar."

Amy just laughs. "I think Edgar's been watching too many of those reality-TV dating shows."

"Or maybe he's just a better observer of life than some of us," I suggest. I, for one, am impressed at his ability to figure all this out. But then, Edgar surprises me in a number of ways.

As it turns out, Edgar is right on the money again. It's really too bad he doesn't bet. But then maybe God doesn't approve of that.

But by the end of the week, it looks like Jordan is still standing on the outside. I guess her one consolation is that she and Timothy are still going together. But, to be honest, I never would've figured that she'd go for a guy like Timothy. I mean, he's nice enough, I guess. But he really doesn't seem like her type. He's kind of loud-mouthed and rowdy and obviously likes being the center of attention. I just never knew that Jordan liked guys like that. Of course, maybe I never knew Jordan at all.

Every time I see Jordan, she is either (1) glommed onto Timothy like super glue, or (2) looking slightly bummed as she walks down the halls by herself. And I'll have to admit she seems pretty lonely. As a result I try to be friendly to her, and I say "Hey" whenever I see her, and I even pause sometimes to ask how she's doing. It's weird though, because she's actually taken the time to speak to me lately, which would've made me deliriously happy before but seems only slightly satisfying now. I suppose it's because I don't *need* her like I used to. Now I just feel sorry for her. Well, sort of.

Okay, the truth is, I sort of think that she's probably just getting what she's asked for. Okay, that might sound mean. But it's how I honestly feel. I mean I never wanted her to get hurt. Okay, maybe I did way back when I was hurting so badly. But I really don't want to see her getting hurt now.

Still, I'm thinking, she *chose* these kids to be her friends, and she knew who they were and what they could do. I'm thinking of all sorts of bad clichés right now. Like she made her bed and has to lie in it, or what goes around comes around. We've been talking about the difference between metaphors and clichés in English and I'm still not sure whether I've got it right or not. But what I'm saying is that Jordan's dilemma seems to be a classic case of getting what you asked for and not liking it in the end.

But, knowing Jordan, I'm sure this whole thing could turn around for her any day now. If she's just patient enough. And I suspect that some of her friends will get bored with their stupid game and just move on. But I could be wrong. Shallow people can be awfully stubborn sometimes.

Anyway, I guess I shouldn't be terribly surprised when Jordan calls me up the following Saturday.

"Hey, what's up, Kara?" she says in her same old cheerful voice. I'm slightly taken aback since it's the exact greeting she always used back when she used to call me, back in the old days when we were still best friends.

"Not much, Jordan. What's up with you?" I am surprised at how easily I fall back into this old pattern. For a moment, it's almost like the past couple of months never even happened. Although I'm fairly certain they did.

"Not much," she answers. "But I was thinking about going to the mall today and wondered if you want to come? I need to get some new shoes."

Naturally, Jordan knows how I love to go shoe shopping. Not that I have a shoe fetish exactly, but I really do like shoes and have pretty good feet for them if I do say so myself. Even so, I'm not so sure I want to hook up with Jordan again. "I don't know," I finally say.

"Oh, come on, Kara," she urges me. "It'll be fun. Just you and me, like old times."

But I'm not so sure I want the old times anymore.

"Look, Kara," she says in a more serious voice. "I know I haven't been much of a friend, but I happen to need a friend now. You know?"

Well, that gets to me and so I agree. "Yeah, sure," I say. "I guess I wasn't doing much of anything anyway."

"Great. I'll pick you up in about an hour. Okay?"

"You drive?" Oh, yeah, I remember. She turned sixteen last month.

Jordan laughs. "Of course, I drive. And now I've even got something to drive."

So I try not to act too surprised, or even impressed, when Jordan shows up in a light blue VW bug. It's not a new one, of course, I know that her parents would never spring for something that expensive. But the fact that it's old only seems to add to its charm.

"This is so cool," I tell her as I climb in.

She grins. "Yeah, it still needs some work though. And I'd like to get the seats redone. But I like it."

I try not to feel jealous. I know God does not want me to be jealous. I know this from reading my new Bible. In fact, it's actually one of the Ten Commandments: do not covet, which is another way of saying "don't be jealous." Plus, I must remind myself, if Jordan and I were still best friends I would be the happiest person on the planet for her. Of course, I would also know that I'd benefit from her car almost as much as she would.

Somehow we manage to make light conversation as she drives to the mall. However, I'm not terribly impressed with her driving abilities and almost yell when she runs a yellow light that's clearly turning red. But I don't.

"I'd be with Timothy today," she says, "but he had to go to a basketball clinic this weekend. All the varsity team is there."

"Oh."

"Did you hear that we have a chance to go to state this year?"

"In football?"

She laughs. That same tinkling laugh, only different somehow. "No, you idiot, I'm not talking about football. We totally suck at football."

"That's what I thought."

"Man, I'll be so glad when this season is over."

"When is that?"

"Couple of weeks."

"Oh." Now I wish I would quit saying "oh." But I just don't seem to have much else to say. This whole experience is feeling a bit surreal and is even starting to unnerve me. Suddenly I realize that I really need to pray. I quickly shoot up a short silent one: *Please, God, show me what to do here.* I'm not even sure what I expect in return, but the idea of connecting to God is a real comfort to me, and before I know it Jordan and I are walking through the mall just like we used to.

It doesn't take long before it all begins to feel like old times, and I almost forget everything that's transpired between us this fall.

After several stores, Jordan finds a very cool pair of shoes and then offers to buy me lunch. I agree, figuring it will be a fair deal since I can tell she's heading straight for the Sushi Bar anyway.

I manage to choke down my sushi, washing it down with a large soda, as I continue to make small talk with Jordan. Mostly I am listening to her going on and on and on about what happened between her and Shawna and Timothy and everyone else who seems to have an opinion about the whole stupid affair. A lot of "she said this . . . " and "he said that . . . " and mostly pretty dull.

"But Timothy was ready to break up with her anyway," Jordan continues. "He said that they'd been history for weeks, but he'd just been putting it off until after the Harvest Dance because he didn't want to hurt Shawna's feelings. I tried to explain that to her, but she just wouldn't listen. It's so unfair the way the kids are acting like I . . . "

But I'm experiencing technical difficulties and am unable to focus on her words after several different versions of the same story. It's just like "blah-blah-blah-blah-blah." She keeps saying the same words over and over again. And it is so painfully boring! Even so, I am slightly stunned. I mean I can't believe that I'm actually sitting here thinking that Jordan Ferguson, my old best friend, is actually this incredibly boring. But she is! At least to me. Now I'm beginning to wonder, *Who's changed here? Her or me?*

Finally, and to my relief, she is ready to go home. "Thanks for coming with me, Kara." She turns and smiles that perfect Jordan smile at me. "I've really missed you. You know, despite everything that's happened, you always were the best friend I ever had."

Now I suppose this should be something of a comfort, but for whatever reason it doesn't feel quite right to me. I can't put my finger on it, but something just doesn't ring true. It's like a pair of shoes that don't quite fit, like they look really cool but they're pinching your toes.

"I'm sorry for the way things went between us," she continues as we get into her car. "I just didn't know how to keep it together with you. I mean it's like you really went out of your way not to fit in with my friends."

"Maybe it's just who I am," I say.

"No, Kara, that's not it. You're cool, really, you are. I know you try to hide it sometimes. And I have to say that since you started hanging with those nerdy kids, well, it's probably even harder to tell. But I know that you're cool. I'm thinking that if you could just get back to who you used to be, and then start hanging with me again . . . well, things could really change for you. You know what I mean?"

I frown now. "I'm not sure. Are you saying you want to be best friends again?"

She shrugs. "Yeah, sure. But you'd have to break it off with your little art club group." She smiles now. "I mean, I realize they're probably nice people and all, but really, Kara, it's time to lose the losers."

I take in a deep breath and hold it. I'm not actually counting to ten, but perhaps that's not such a bad idea. Then it occurs to me that I probably don't really need to get angry at Jordan. Maybe it's just a God thing, or maybe I'm growing up. But I'm thinking it won't accomplish anything to explode on her. After all, she's only doing what she knows how to do best — be her superficial self.

"You know, Jordan," I begin slowly, calmly. "I happen to like where my life is right now. And I like my new friends too."

She turns and looks at me, almost running into the back of a car as she does.

"Look out!" I scream and brace myself as she stamps on the brakes and screeches to a stop just in time.

"Sorry," she says. "Guess I better watch the road. But what did you just say? Did you say that you actually *like* your nerdy friends?"

"I don't think of them as nerdy, Jordan. I think of them as interesting and nice. And, yes, I do like them. A lot."

"You're kidding, right?" She glances my way then back to her driving, which is a relief since I really don't want to end up in the hospital today.

"No, I'm not," I say in a firm voice. I notice she's frowning now and I suspect I've hurt her feelings and I feel a little bit guilty. "But I like you too, Jordan, and I'd still like to be your friend. I've really missed you, and your family too. We spent a lot of great years together, you know."

She nods. "I know. And I've missed you too. And I'd really like us to be friends again. To be honest, it's been kind of lonely lately. I mean Timothy is great and all, but he's not always that available. And he's got sports and stuff. I really need a girlfriend to hang with too."

"I know what you mean." I'm thinking of Edgar now. He's a good friend, but sometimes I almost wish he was a girl. Almost.

"And so maybe we can work this thing out," she says in a happy voice. I notice that she forgets to use her turn signal as she turns down the street to our apartment complex. "But, you'd have to understand that you can't have it both ways, Kara. I mean you'd really need to lose the losers. I'm not kidding about that."

"Neither am I," I tell her. "I can't give up my friends."

"*Why not?*" She pulls in front of the apartments in a fast stop and jerks on the emergency brake. "It's not like any of them are really your best friend, Kara. I mean, whether you know it or not, I watch you guys sometimes and I can tell. Felicia is best friends with Jessie Rubenstein, and that Amy, well, God only knows who she's best friends with, but I assure you, it's not you. And certainly that Edgar creep couldn't be your—"

"*Excuse* me!" I interrupt in a fairly loud voice. "But Edgar is *not* a creep. He's a very good friend. You're right, he's not my *best* friend, but he's a very good friend."

"Fine, whatever." She turns and looks at me, clearly exasperated now. "My point is you don't *have* a best friend, Kara. And neither do I. And I think that—"

"Wait a minute," I say, holding my hands up to stop her. "That's *not* true. I *do* have a best friend."

She gives me her famous skeptical look now. One brow up, one brow down. Oh, how well I know it. "You honestly have a best friend, do you? Well then, who is it?"

"Jesus," I say in a calm voice. Surprisingly calm. I am actually impressed.

Now she looks totally stunned. She stares at me as if I've completely lost my mind. "You've gotta be kidding."

I shake my head.

"You're totally joking now, aren't you? This is a joke. Right?"

"Wrong. It's the truth. I invited Jesus into my heart, partly because I was so lonely. But when he came inside of me I realized that he's the best friend I could ever have."

"No way!"

"Way."

"This is too bizarre, Kara. Are you actually saying that Jesus Christ is your *best* friend? I mean, I go to church and I believe in God. But how on earth can Jesus be your best friend? Get real."

Well, I try to explain it to her, but it becomes quite clear that she really doesn't want to listen. Finally, I give up. "Look, Jordan, this is just the way it is, okay? Jesus really is my best friend. And I happen to like the other friends I have too. And I'm happy to be your friend again. But I seriously doubt that we'll ever be best friends. At least not under your conditions." I open the car door now. Jordan looks completely baffled, as if she cannot believe that I'm actually turning down the fantastic opportunity to be the best friend of Jordan Ferguson, cheerleader and basic cool girl. But the fact is I am. And I'm totally happy about it!

"Sorry to disappoint you," I tell her. "And I hope things work out with you and your new friends. But if they don't, there's always someone waiting to be your best friend, Jordan. And, believe me, he's a friend who will never let you down."

"Whatever." She rolls her eyes and revs her engine now and I can tell she's impatient to go.

"Take care," I tell her. "And keep your eyes on the road."

"Yeah, sure." She shakes her head at me. "Have a nice life, Kara."

"Thanks, I am." I close the door just in time for her to peel out, which really looks ridiculous in an old VW bug, and I feel sorry for her tires since they already look somewhat threadbare to me.

As I go up the stairs to the apartment, I can't help but feel sorry for Jordan too. And I know that I'll be praying for her more than ever now. I guess I never realized just how needy she really is. I probably never would've either, if she hadn't dumped me.

I smile to myself as I slip my key into the lock on the door. It suddenly occurs to me that God knew what he was doing all along. All the crud that I went through, all the pain and suffering—the loneliness. I think it was definitely worth it.

Thank you, Jesus! I pray. *Thanks for being my BEST FRIEND.*

reader's guide

1. Kara and Jordan had been friends since kindergarten, but how would you describe their friendship? Tight? Shallow? Dependable? Unbalanced?

2. Although they'd been friends for years, do you think Kara and Jordan knew each other as well as they thought they did? Why or why not?

3. Kara was so devastated after Jordan dumped her. What was she dependent on Jordan's friendship for? Why do you think she relied on the friendship so much for these things?

4. How would you describe a good friend? What qualities do you look for in your own friends?

5. What makes a friend trustworthy? Untrustworthy?

6. In your experience, do friends take on certain roles in friend-ships? (In other words, does one usually have more power or influence than the other?) Why do you think this is? Can this ever change? How?

7. Can friends outgrow each other? Is it okay to move on? Explain.

8. Is any friendship strong enough to last forever? What would make a friendship that strong?

9. What's most important to you: Friends? Family? God? Your dog?

10. Do you believe that Jesus can be your best friend? Is it true that he'll never let you down or dump you for another? Can you trust him with your heart? Explain why or why not.

TrueColors Book 2:
Deep Green

Coming in April 2004

The story of two girls who both want one guy, and the choices that hurt them and heal them along the way.

One

I KNOW WHAT EVERYONE'S BEEN SAYING ABOUT ME, BUT IT'S NOT MY FAULT that Timothy Lawrence dumped Shawna Frye the day after the Harvest Dance. Really, it's just the way life goes sometimes. I mean just because you've gone with a guy for a year doesn't mean you own him heart and soul. And I didn't see any engagement ring on Shawna's finger. She swears Timothy got her a promise ring once, but she claims she lost it swimming at the lake last summer. I'm not sure if I believe her. Especially since Shawna is saying all kinds of things these days. Mostly about me. And mostly untrue, not to mention unkind.

"That Jordan Ferguson is a backstabbing tramp," I overheard her tell Lucy Farrell in the locker room today. Naturally, she didn't realize that I could hear her going on and on from behind my closed door of the bathroom stall. Or maybe she did. Maybe she just didn't care that her words cut me deeply. Of course, everyone knows that she wants to hurt me. I'm just glad that she's not the violent type or I'd have to be watching my backside. At least I don't think she is. But why she was telling all this to Lucy Farrell, who's really not even involved in our group, is totally beyond me. Not that Lucy's not nice, she is. But it's really not any of her business. I suspect Shawna's just looking for new sets of ears, since everyone else is probably getting sick and tired of hearing her whine and complain about me all the time.

The really sad part is that I honestly thought Shawna and I were friends. Good friends even. And I really liked her. Next to my old best friend, Kara Hendricks, Shawna was the best friend I'd ever had. She's fun and funny, and we're both cheerleaders and have the exact same taste (including boys, as it turns out), but I'd really hoped we could be friends for a long, long time.

"Didn't you think she'd get mad when you stole her boyfriend?" Amber Elliot asked me the other day. I could tell she was looking at me like I was the village idiot. Like, *Duh, how dumb are you, Jordan Ferguson?*

But the truth is I didn't. "I told you that Timothy said they were over with," I explained to Amber in my most convincing tone. "He said that they both knew their relationship was history and that they were only staying together until the Harvest Dance, and only because he'd promised to take her to it."

"That's not what Shawna says," said Amber with eyes that still looked doubtful.

Now the really hard part here is that I'm the new girl in the group. And everyone is loyal to Shawna. And most of them are siding with her already. Amber's the only one who's been trying to stay in the middle ground, but that might have more to do with being head cheerleader than with being my friend. Still, I haven't given up on her. "What do you think I should do?" I asked her. "Should I break up with Timothy?" Of course, I knew that no matter what she said that I wouldn't do this, couldn't do this. But I was curious as to how she would respond.

"I don't know," she said. "But you and Shawna better sort this all out before basketball season starts. We can't have two snarling cheerleaders spoiling everything for everyone else."

I forced my best smile. "I'm trying, Amber, really I am. But Shawna won't even speak to me."

"Well, give her time to chill." Amber rolled her eyes dramatically. "Thank goodness football season is almost over with."

"And Tim says that basketball season is supposed to be really good," I said, hoping to encourage her.

"Yeah, it's supposed to be. Let's just hope the cheerleaders can do their part to keep it together without murdering each other before the season is over." She shook her head as if I was personally responsible for the morale of the entire team. "I gotta go now."

I waved goodbye and wished I had said something more convincing. I mean, I could really use someone like Amber to be solidly on my side. The truth is I feel pretty alone right now. Even Kara Hendricks, my old best friend, seems to be holding me at arm's length these days. But at least I have my Timothy. That's some consolation prize!

And I can't deny that I've had the hots for Tim ever since last year. He was a junior then, but already playing on the varsity basketball team, since he's that good. Naturally, he didn't even know that I existed back then. But I still enjoyed watching him from a distance. I used to cheer for him from the bleachers like he was the only one down there. And he looked totally awesome in his blue and red uniform, and I really liked watching him dribble that ball down the court with style and grace. Most of all I liked his smile. I still do.

Of course, I never told anyone this. Not even Kara. My feeling is that when you really, really like someone, it's best to play your cards close to your chest (as my dad would say). It gives you the advantage. And I think that has a lot to do with how I managed to hook Timothy too. I acted pretty nonchalant toward him. Like I could take him or leave him. I laughed lightly at his jokes, but then gave it right back to him as if I didn't care what he thought about me. But the truth is, I did. I did a lot.

And then when he asked me to dance with him at the Harvest Dance, since everyone else was sort of switching partners. I just acted all aloof, and like, well, okay, I suppose I could dance with you. Kind of like hard to get. And he kept getting more and more interested.

"I don't ever remember seeing you around school," he told me as we danced a slow dance. "Until you made cheerleader anyway. So where were you hiding all this time?"

I shrugged. "I've been around."

And so it went. A regular cat-and-mouse game. But he thought he was the cat pursuing the mouse. Little did he know.

Still, I never really dreamed that he would pursue me seriously. At least not so quickly anyway. But the very next day he called me up and then came over to my house. He told me that he'd been postponing his breakup with Shawna, but that the time had finally come. He seemed slightly disturbed about the whole thing, which I thought was rather sweet and endearing. But I tried to console him and assure him that if it was really the time to break up, the best thing was to just do it, and do it as quickly and painlessly as possible.

Maybe I was wrong about that.

about the author

MELODY CARLSON has written dozens of books for all age groups, but she particularly enjoys writing for teens. Perhaps this is because her own teen years remain so vivid in her memory. After claiming to be an atheist at the ripe old age of twelve, she later surrendered her heart to Jesus and has been following him ever since. Her hope and prayer for all her readers is that each one would be touched by God in a special way through her stories. For more information, please visit Melody's website at www.melodycarlson.com.

Pitch Black: Color Me Lost
Morgan Bergstrom thinks her life is as bad as it can get, but it's about to get a whole lot worse. Her close friend Jason Harding has just killed himself, and no one knows why. As she struggles with her grief, Morgan must make her life's ultimate decision — before it's too late.
1-57683-532-4

Burnt Orange: Color Me Wasted
Amber Conrad has a problem: Her youth group friends Simi and Lisa won't get off her case about the drinking parties she's been going to. Everyone does it. What's the big deal? Will she be honest with herself and her friends before things really get out of control?
1-57683-533-2

Fool's Gold: Color Me Consumed
On furlough from Papua New Guinea, Hannah Johnson spends some time with her Prada-wearing cousin, Vanessa. Hannah feels like an alien around her host — everything Vanessa has is so nice. Hannah knows that stuff's not supposed to matter, but why does she feel a twinge of jealousy deep down inside?
1-57683-534-0

Blade Silver: Color Me Scarred
As Ruth Wallace attempts to stop cutting, her family life deteriorates further to the point that she isn't sure she'll ever be able to stop. Ruth needs help, but will she get it before this habit threatens her life?
1-57683-535-9

Bitter Rose: Color Me Crushed
Maggie's parents suddenly split up after twenty-five years of marriage. The whole situation has Maggie feeling hurt, distraught, and, most of all, violently bitter. She's near desperate for someone who can restore her confidence in love.
1-57683-536-7

Faded Denim: Color Me Trapped
Emily hates her overweight body, her insecure personality, and sometimes even her "perfect" friends. She takes drastic measures to change her body, but the real issues are weighing down her heavy heart.
1-57683-537-5

Bright Purple: Color Me Confused
Ramie Grant cannot believe it when her best friend, Jessica, tells her she's a homosexual. It's just a matter of time before others on the basketball team find out. Quickly, little jokes become vicious attacks. In the end, Ramie must decide if she will stand by Jessica's side or turn her back on a friend in need.
1-57683-950-8

Moon White: Color Me Enchanted
All spirituality is good, right? So says Heather, a teenage girl-next-door, who has recently begun studying the traditions of Wicca. Yet she soon learns that her "harmless" spiritual journey is anything but. In her darkest moment, she discovers hope in a long-lost letter that reconnects her to the truth she's been searching for all along.
1-57683-951-6